CHAPTER ONE

For a footloose ex-Ranger who'd come out of that fight at the Hashknife with a bullet-made limp and some nightmare memories of Mossman's resolve to clean up this Territory, I guess you could say I had heard the owl hoot. Several wasted years had gone down the drain since Cap Mossman had turned in his badge and taken up ranching over in New Mexico and I had quit, too, to drift back to Half Step and a humdrum life of trading heirlooms for cash.

Broiling glare of the Arizona sun was scarce two hours from dropping back of the mountain when I rode into the plaza at Ajo.

The bad boys were beginning to ease back into this country, in spite of the Rangers, now that old Burt wasn't around to harass them. Once again gun sound was banging through the hills and dealing with tame Injuns made me think more than once of signing up for another hitch, bad leg and all. As one of Mossman's Rangers I'd come to spot

1

the breed soon as I laid eyes on them and like an old fire horse I could feel the pull of remembered excitement.

I had taken in most everything in sight time I pulled up Gretchen by the hitchrail fronting the assayer's office. Ajo was mining with a capital M. Cow outfits were in town, a sure sign of payday. Wasn't no big crowd lallygaggin' in the plaza, but tied horses and buckboards was thicker than flies on a spill of sorghum. I'd been aiming to get back to Half Step and tell my old man I wasn't cut out to be no counter-jumper, that routine chores couldn't never make up for the kind of a life I'd known with Burt Mossman.

To tell the plain truth I was bored plumb silly.

Getting out Durham and papers while slanching around one more cautious look I twisted up a smoke and set fire to it, rummaging my mind what I had better do next. I could eat and push on or—willing to risk a bit—could spend the night here and slip away first thing in the morning. What I purely wanted was to get myself home.

I hauled my weight into the saddle, ignoring the dubious look Gretchen flung me. Off to the left about a whoop and a holler was a near bleached-out sign spelling LIVERY;

and that's where we ambled, up a gut-narrow alley that presently fetched us to a barn's hoof-tracked ramp.

An old duffer reluctantly got up off his peach crate. "Yeah? By the week or the night?"

"Expect one night'll take care of our needs. Give this animal a good feed of oats. Rub her down—proper." I peered around. "All right if she swipes a drink from that trough?"

"What it's there fer. Two bits ever' time she lowers her head."

"Water must be a heap scarce in this community."

I could see he was fixing to get on his dignity. "Never mind. She's worth it," I grumbled, and flipped him a cartwheel. "Where's the nearest grub for a two-legged specimen?"

"Buck, two doors down, can take care of your tapeworm."

Racked by saddle cramp I took myself back to the alley mouth, crushed the butt under a bootheel and stretched another long glance the full length of the square without latching onto anything to put my wind up. Place he'd touted said BUSTED CROCK, a two-by-four hash house right next to the stage office.

Getting out of my brush jacket, I slapped out the dust against the nearest wall. My gimpy leg was giving me hell; bullet holes don't cure up like an overnight cough . . . unfortunate. I didn't see anything showed a need to squat and reach. Place would liven up before long without any prodding. A few of those old varmints we hadn't shot and buried might recollect my face; something I'd forever have to be watching out for.

I mounted the porch and went on inside.

Five-six shapes held down stools at the counter. Only table occupied was in a corner by the window. A woman sat there over a half-finished meal. Preempting another half-way down the long room, I gave my order to the biscuit-shooter and made a careful point of minding my own business.

Carving up my steak, cramming my gut with frijoles, I couldn't escape the scrutiny I was getting from that dame, the feel of her probing my face, sorting out the rest of me. I put up with it long as I could and then, shelling out some silver, shoved back my chair and headed for the door.

Her heels tap-tapped behind me and I

swung round on the porch with a smothered oath.

She put a hand on my elbow. "I'm Fern Larrimore. Could I speak with you a minute?"

I gave her a scowl, not wanting any part of this. "I don't usually," she said, "approach strange men in this fashion."

"All right. Let's get away from this door."

We moved down onto the walk, her arm slipped through mine. Not like a hustler, more like she had it in mind I might try to get away. "Would you tell me your name?"

"Corrigan—Brice Corrigan." We stopped in front of the stage office. "What's the problem?"

"That's just it." She looked at me undecided and puzzled. "I don't really know. It's just a feeling I have. Would you be free to take a job?"

"What job?"

"A sort of watching brief. You see, my brother's an anthropologist—interprets fossils and relics. He had a couple of months' leave from the university to see what he can turn up about those old cliff dwellers, the faraway ancestors of today's Pueblo Indians. Specifically the Basketmakers—"

"I wouldn't know a Basketmaker if one jumped up and bit me."

A quick and brief grin streaked across the contours of that scrubbed-clean face. "You have the look of belonging. Jeff—my brother —has to have a guide, he knows nothing about this part of the country. He's out here to make a dig, nothing elaborate, a kind of probe is all, to see if there's anything here to be found. I'd like to hire you."

"I don't want to be hired. I'm trying to get home."

"Is your home around here?"

"No."

Her blue-green eyes kept trying to take me apart. A sigh came out of her. "Look—" she said, "I've an uneasy feeling we're going to need more help than my brother is counting on. . . . Whatever your business is, whatever your stipend, I'll double it."

I stared at her, astonished, yanked my glance off her face to throw another look around. More horse sound, more jabber, more movement in the plaza, more people sifting around and about over the rough plank walks. No ore wagons in sight but plenty of ranch rigs, a lot more jaspers standing around by the tie rails. I eyed the look of her again. Younger than I'd reckoned.

6

Not much more than twenty, well built but no beauty. "Why me?"

"Sometimes," she said, "you have to fight fire with fire."

She had a pretty sharp eye for a girl her age and a dude at that. She had me picked for a bravo, I could see that plain enough. "Figurin' to buy a . . ." I let it go, to say, disgusted, "This thing your brother's after. Some kind of loot, is it—buried plunder, that sort of thing?"

A rush of color came into her look, flushing some of the paleness out of her cheeks. A touch of resentment sharpened her voice. "Of course not! I've told you; he's an anthropology major, an assistant professor at a Chicago university. He's hunting for Indian artifacts, to learn whatever he can, to pin down the time these cliff dwellers arrived here from Asia and Siberia, the length of their stay and why they aren't still here. That sort of thing. This is very important. We want to know what their day-to-day life was like."

She said, more composed, "Jeff's got hold of a man called Harry Hatcher who grew up in this territory, knows all about it. Mr. Hatcher's going to show us the best places for a dig. He's told Jeff about some caves

7

that have petroglyphs—he's been on digs before, understands what is needed. It's the men Hatcher's hired that makes me uneasy."

"This Hatcher, what do you know about him?"

"Only what Jeff learned from the bank—"

"Bank, eh? Bank vouch for him? Guarantee him, did they?"

"Not exactly. They say he's been a guide, takes out hunting parties. Took a party of archaeologists into the Tonto Basin—"

"And where is he proposing to take your brother?"

"Into the Chaco Canyon country."

"Pretty well into the back of beyond. Damn rough country, lady. No place to be draggin' a woman through—"

"Yes. That's what he said."

"But you aim to go anyhow."

"That's right. I've got a stake in this."

"Don't sound much like a woman's business. I wouldn't expect your brother would care to put you at risk. Let me get this straight. As I understand it, the reason you want to rope me in is because you don't like the kind of crew Hatcher's put together—"

"It's not so much the crew I dislike. It's this fellow Fletcher and another called Clampas. I don't like the looks of them."

"Have you told your brother?" I said. "What is it with you? Can't you talk to him?"

"I've told them both—him and Hatcher. Jeff only throws up his hands. 'Women's notions' he calls everything I point out. Hatcher says we have to understand this place where we're going is bleak, rough country, a maze of draws and ridges where anything could happen—wild and desolate. He thinks we might run into fugitives, rene-gades, even hostile Indians. He says we need men like Clampas and Fletcher as a kind of insurance. Jeff calls them 'rough diamond.' He thinks it's all in my head."

"I don't think they'll want me along in that case."

Her chin came up. "Perhaps not, but I'm the one who is putting up the most of the money for this dig—my inheritance. Without my support there won't be any dig."

I looked her over again. I blew out my breath. "Lady," I said, "I've got to get home. I been away too long now."

She met my stare with a kind no man cares to get from a female. "Have I been wrong about you?"

CHAPTER TWO

She had me there, no two ways about it.

Man could be a rightdown bastard, yet even the worst had to have some value of self to hang on to. Graveled me plenty to be pushed and shoved by the likes of this kid who had nothing I wanted and wasn't no better looking than the handful of others I'd left wailing in the past.

"Shit!" I said, and didn't care that she heard it. I felt meaner than gar soup thickened with tadpoles, too damned riled to keep a hitch on my lip. "Ain't it crossed your mind latchin' on to me could be jumpin' from the skillet straight into the fire?"

Just breath wasted. I said, "This brother of yours—where-at will I find him?"

She half turned, lifting an arm with the ghost of a smile. "Over there at the hotel. With Harry. You going to play this my way?"

I charged off through the clutter of horses and wagons, too disgruntled to answer. She could think what she liked and to hell with her. I felt like a fool being choused around this way.

She wasn't two steps behind when I reached the far walk and stepped onto the hotel veranda, hating to think what damage this fine brother of hers could do pawing around in his greed for more facts. "Dudes!" I muttered, but this Larrimore filly with her mop of roan hair had a lot more to her than appeared on the surface.

I paused to say grimly, "Aside from this Hatcher, big brother, yourself and that pair you don't cotton to, how many others is roped into this deal? What's the size of your crew?"

"Well . . . let's see. Hatcher's picked up four men—"

"With me—if I go into this, that makes an all-over total of ten in this party?"

"Twelve, counting the Mexican handyman and cook."

I looked down at the dog sitting patient by her legs, a shaggy mixed breed of some sort, black and tan. "That dog goin' too?"

"Flossie? Certainly. I sometimes think she has more sense than my brother."

"This Hatcher, now. What do you think of him?"

"He's all right, I guess." She pushed hair off her cheek. "A little glib perhaps. Seems very knowledgeable, easy to get along with."

"Yeah. I bet. Who's assembling the supplies, the stuff you'll have to pack into that country?"

"Hatcher has that all taken care of. We're planning to leave first thing in the morning." Her glance swung up, openly curious. "Are we likely to meet the sort of riffraff Harry mentioned?"

"Can't tell what you'll meet up with these days. There's riffraff anyplace. Far as Indians go there's actually no saying. Some of them's gettin' a mite touchy here of late. Come on, let's get at it."

I limped after her into the lobby. Stuffed animal heads decorated the walls. The floor held a scatter of Navajo rugs; club chairs were grouped about an oversize fireplace, and three paunchy gents in the garb of ranch owners had their heads together off in a far corner. Girl led the way toward worn leather chairs where two men leaning forward were engaged in what appeared to be an earnest conversation. They looked around as we approached. The one I reckoned to be Hatcher stood up fairly pleasant as Fern stopped in front of them.

"Jeff, I want you to meet Brice Corrigan, who'll be going our way. Brice, this is my brother, Jeff Larrimore. From Chicago."

Larrimore said, getting onto his feet some-what surprised, "Glad to know you, Brice," and put out a hand, which I shook as a matter of simple courtesy. "Do you live around here?" he asked, curious, civil.

"Not too near, I'm afraid. My old man runs the trading post at Half Step."

His eyes changed a little but hung on to his smile. "That so? We're going north for a tour through the Basketmaker country, looking up the remains of what these Nava-jos call the Ancient Ones. University is spon-soring a kind of small dig."

"Big country." I nodded. "Rougher'n a cob."

"And this," Fern said brightly, "is Harry Hatcher, who will be in charge of the route and our crew."

"You been at Half Step long?" Hatcher inquired, shaking my paw.

"Born there."

"How are the natives around those parts? Any truth in the rumors I hear going around?"

"Could be. Some of them seem a mite restless lately. But I don't figure any trouble you run into can be charged up to natives. Renegades," I tucked in, "ain't confined to one color."

"True enough." He laughed. "Arizona's got their share all right. Did I understand Fern to say you're also heading north?"

"He's going with us," she put in without beating around any bushes. "I've hired him to round out our safari."

Through what had the makings of an awkward silence Harry Hatcher said with no loss of charm, "Glad to have you with us, Corrigan. Bigger the party the more likely we'll be to come through in one piece." Behind his bland mask he was giving the look of me a thorough going-over.

"You expectin' trouble?"

"Not at all," he assured us with a comforting smile. "Just one of them fellers feels it pays to be prepared."

Bobbing his head, Larrimore chipped in. "Harry's been around. I haven't turned up one person since I've been out here who knows as much as he does about the people we're trying to find—the Anasazi. All the Indians I've talked to just look at you and shrug. They don't know the first thing about those old cliff dwellers."

"Understandable." Hatcher nodded, confident smile enveloping Fern. "They have no written history, no way of bridging the gap of centuries. For all practical purposes the folks Jeff's interested in disappeared from this region about 1400 B.C., give or take a handful of fortnights," he said, much admiring his own wit, it seemed like. "I'm going to take him back where probably no other whites have ever been, right into the heart of that Basketmaker country."

He had the right line to take with young Larrimore. Fern's brother looked pleased as a cat with a fine plump bird by the tail. "Yes," he told me, "quite a bit of serious work has been done on the Pueblo peoples but they came later. First pueblo we know about has been dated no later than seven hundred and fifty, and that's after Christ. Practically modern compared with the aboriginal people I'm trying to get a line on.

"You see, what we need is more artifacts. We've a great need to understand more about primitive man. These Basketmakers come fairly close to being as near as we can get to early man in this country," he declared with conviction. "Near as we know now, they arrived here from what we call Siberia either during or immediately after the Ice Age."

Hatcher with his smile appeared to be in full agreement. "What we're trying to do here is a lot like hunting for the Missing

Link, with apologies to Darwin. So little, truly, has been discovered you could practically"—he chuckled—"put the whole bundle in a teacup. Jeff hopes to embark on a voyage of discovery, wants to pioneer the forgotten world of the Anasazi and go straight back some twenty-five thousand years!"

Yep. You had to hand it to Harry. He'd come as near in tune with Larrimore as two peas out of the same pod. I thought to see right then at least a partial reason for the girl's disquiet. I wouldn't trust this Hatcher half as far as I could heave him. "Just what," I asked Larrimore, "are you hopin' to find?"

"If we can get onto the right location, I believe there's a possibility we can unearth some primitive tools and weapons, bones of prehistoric animals they've killed, artifacts used by them in everyday living—that sort of thing. The scientific community, the anthropologists and scholars, so far as these people are concerned, haven't managed to come up with the definitive answer."

Hatcher said, "We'd like to be able to pin down the source of whatever it was that drove these folks here from their former homelands. From wherever they came from, be it fire, floods, famine, pestilence, drought or whatever. An ambitious concept? Certainly. But Jeff feels strongly if he can come onto remains that haven't been tampered with—"

Larrimore cut in, fairly bubbling with excitement. "Harry thinks he can put me onto some graves."

"Where?"

"If I remember correct," Hatcher said persuasively, "it's someplace in the vicinity of Chaco Canyon. Lot of cliff dwellings back in that cut-up country."

"Cliff dwellings, sure," I said. "I don't remember any graves. I went through there several months ago."

Harry showed his smoothest smile. "You didn't get back far enough. There's places back there no white man's ever seen—"

"And what do *you* expect to get out of all this?"

Hatcher laughed. "Maybe I'd like a little piece of the credit when Jeff makes his big find. That's reasonable, ain't it?"

"You'll have it," Jeff said earnestly. "This could be a big thing!" He pulled in a gusty breath. "The pots, pans and bones of man's culture. Going back pretty near to the beginning!"

I hadn't no doubt he was sold on it, but

Hatcher to me didn't seem hardly the kind to give a whoop about credit. He had to be in this for something more substantial if I knew anything about the cut of his jib.

The dog sprawled at Fern's feet had the look of watching Harry with a jaundiced eye, too. Larrimore, still flushed with enthusiasm, bit off the end and lit up a thin cigar he produced from a pocket of his silver-buttoned vest. "If we could get even one absolutely conclusive answer—"

"I think we've talked enough," Fern said. "This place is filling up. If you fellows expect to eat, you had better get a move on."

Harry nodded. "I guess we've got the subject pretty well covered. "If you're goin' with us on this jaunt," he said in my direction, "be down at the corrals by five o'clock tomorrow morning to help us load. Jeff's counting on an early start."

That broke up the conference. The girl, the dog and young Larrimore moved away.

Thinking a drink would go pretty good right then, I was turning around to go hunt up one when Hatcher thrust out a hand. "Let me ask you somethin', Corrigan. How'd you manage to work yourself into this?" His eyes, bright and hard, locked into mine. "Where'd you meet up with that girl?"

He plainly didn't like the way I grinned. "You look like a saddle tramp—a damn grubline rider!"

"Reckon that was it," I said. "Miss Larrimore's got a heap of compassion. Offered me a job, she did. An' being chock full of pity myself, I signed on. Just as simple as that."

To keep an eye on Gretchen—make sure she wasn't tampered with—I talked myself into a deal with the livery keeper that got me the right to bed down in his hay-filled loft. I must've tossed and turned pretty near the whole night. Too many questions, too few answers, too many faces flitting through my head. I hadn't met the pair of hombres that had driven the girl into taking me on . . .

My thoughts jumped around to Burt Mossman. People claimed Arizona Rangers never looked back, but Burt was one who stuck to a trail like heelflies after a fresh-butchered calf. And I was mighty sure, too, Harry Hatcher hadn't missed my occasional limp. In this much time that leg should have cured itself. There was a heap of talk these days—and a heap of agitation, about this Territory getting to be a state.

A good few of the pictures flitting through my mind had to do with Fern Larrimore and this thing I had let her auger me into. Hell, a kid in three-cornered pants ought to've had more sense than let himself be prodded into this kind of trap!

No one had to tell me a ranny like Hatcher didn't give two snorts for Jeff Larrimore's Injun ancestors. Nor for Fern. No girl could compete with the kind of return that slick catamount was hunting! What he saw in this deal had to be real dinero, and scratch around as I would and damn sure did, I couldn't see big mazuma in old bones and pot shards.

I got down next morning to the corrals ahead of schedule, aiming to have me a plumb thorough look at what kind of a crew handsome Harry had picked up to make sure this deal went the way he intended. I saw with disgust there wasn't no answer there. Four of these five hombres was just ordinary cowhands of the twenty-five-dollar-a-month sort. The fifth, Turtle Jones, might be a cut above them, both in gumption and savvy, which to my way of thinking wasn't saying a whole heap. The other pair—the ones that had got Fern's wind up—was a different breed of cats, a breed I knew from the bootheels up.

Fletcher turned up first with a jingle and scrape of bigroweled spurs. His look showed the hardness long years had ground into him. Pale flaxen hair beneath a squaw man's hat and pale blue peepers above his sneering mouth. A short-barreled .44 was shoved into his waistband and he came striding through the crew like he owned the whole shebang. "What the bloody hell," he rasped at me, "d'you think you're doin' here?"

"Hadn't given it much thought. You the boss of this outfit?"

He stood like a coiled spring, tipped forward, hands working with his mouth pinched into a tight-rimmed slit. "That's Corrigan, Fletcher—new man we've signed on," Hatcher called. "Get off your high horse and help stow these packs."

"You hire him?"

"He was hired by Miss Larrimore and don't you forget it. Now quit pawing sod and get busy." Hatcher turned away to speak to a man who had just come into the corral where the pack string was being loaded with boxes and bulging gunnysacks. "Keep your eye on that fool. I want no trouble round here!" Then off Hatcher went, all smiles, to

21

greet the Larrimores, who had just come up with their saddled mounts.

"Reckon you must be Clampas," I said to the man Harry's spoken to. "Looks like we'll have a good day to get off on. I'm the new hand—Corrigan."

This Clampas—if that's who he was— would have had to stand twice to cast one shadow, so thin he was, so tall and gangling with that flat tough face above the wipe at his throat and the six-shooter slung at either hip. The gaunt cheeks twitched, amber eyes crawled over me like fingers and he flung away with a bridled impatience, never opening his mouth.

No wonder, I thought, the girl was uneasy. That pair was no kind to stamp your boot and yell *boo!* at.

I slanched a look round for Fletcher as Fern's black dog came sidling over to test the air at my legs. Reaching a hand down for sniffing, I heard Clampas demand of Hatcher in a grumbling growl, "How come that waddy ain't helpin' the boys load?" I didn't catch Harry's answer because just then Fern, stopping beside me, said, "Where's your mount?"

I cocked my head to where Gretchen stood on grounded reins. The girl's face showed a considerable astonishment. "You surely must be teasing. Nobody rides *mules!*"

"I been ridin' this one a heap of dry miles."

She stared, disbelieving. Even when I mentioned the mule and me went together and she couldn't have one without having the other, she couldn't seem to take it in. Gretchen waggled both ears in obvious approval and heaved up a sigh like a bunch of hailstones coming off a tin roof. Fern had to laugh.

I said, "Where's the cook?"

"Backed out." She looked provoked.

"Expect we'll manage to make do if we put our minds to it." I sent a look at the overhead. All along the horizon the gray blank of sky was taking on a pinkish tinge. We watched Fletcher and Clampas ride out of the corral. "You don't truly think"—it come out too solemn—"I'm whacked from the same bit of goods as that pair?"

She got into her saddle and sat looking down at me. You had to like the way she wrinkled up her nose. "Expect we'll just have to wait and see, won't we?"

I knew her eyes were laughing but reckoned to glimpse a suggestion of warmth that hadn't been there before. Bitterly damning

23

the notion, I sent an irritable hand across new-shaven chin and told myself there was enough on my plate without indulging that sort of foolishness.

Fletcher and Clampas rode off into the brush, the crew with the pack string swinging in behind, followed by Hatcher and the Chicago professor, young Jeff got up like Montgomery Ward's version of what the well-dressed Western gentleman will be wearing this fall. "Don't you think he looks real nice?" Fern asked.

Eyeing the flat-topped hat, white shirt, red tie, that cowhide vest with double row of silver buttons, sand-colored whipcord pants stuffed into knee-high boots with hugeroweled shiny nickel-plated spurs, I could only wonder.

"Very nice," I told her. "Time to get crackin'." Then I climbed onto Gretchen.

We went along in this strung-out fashion for maybe half an hour without no more gab.

Then abruptly she said, "What sort of work were you doing before we ran across each other—I mean, were you working for one of these ranches?"

"I was headin' for home."

"And before that?"

"Oh . . . a little of this and some of that."

"You aren't very forthcoming, Corrigan."

"Ain't much I can say. Most of the time, like now, I been ridin' for a livin'."

Her glance was like a pair of hands digging into me. "Would you describe yourself," she persisted, "as—"

"Mostly I been what you might call fiddle-footed. Haven't stayed too long anyplace, I reckon."

"Tell me about your home. Was someone ill that you wanted to hurry back?"

"Reckon," I said, "they're healthy enough. I wasn't hurryin' particular, I just wanted to get there. Matter of fact I never knew my mother; goin' by what I've heard I guess she died pretty young. Old man's all right, never been sick a day in his life."

"Doesn't he get pretty lonesome?"

"Not that I ever noticed. Runnin' that tradin' post don't leave much time for lonesome."

"What does he sell?"

"Anything folks'll buy, I reckon: beads, food, flashy gewgaws, blankets—that kinda stuff."

"Doesn't he sell whiskey?"

"Not to Indians he don't!"

"Well, you needn't take my head off about it."

"They got a law against that. My old man wouldn't want to lose his license. Or any other privilege, come to that."

I could feel her studying eyes going over me. "I have noticed," she said, "when you're not thinking about it you have a tendency to limp. An old hurt perhaps?"

"The leg got bit by a bullet."

Expect it come to her goddam notice the conversation was definitely adjourned. She rode off after her brother, who rode alone up ahead of us.

Country was beginning to show its teeth a bit now, not yet what you'd call rough but increasingly cluttered with rocks and such barbed growth as mesquite, yucca, Spanish bayonet and wolf's candle. An occasional saguaro reared its spiny length some thirty or more feet into the rapidly heating air above this sandy floor. The sharp spikes of hedgehog with their curled-up crimson blooms were generously mixed among the prickly pear, cholla, fishhooks and barrel cactus. I'd been living with such for the past couple weeks and paid them scant heed other than to yank the blue wipe up across my nose in the hope of filtering out some of the dust.

After a couple hours of reasonable progress young Larrimore in his grit-covered finery dropped back to share some chunks of his learning about things nearest to his heart, in especial the long-gone Anasazi, mainly Basketmakers of the earliest variety.

I said, "Let's hope you don't run into any chindis."

"What's that?" he questioned, twisting around to eye me, curious.

"Chindis," I told him, "are what Navajos call the spirits of the dead."

He gave that some study, considerable more than you might reckon it warranted. "But the Navajos aren't related to the cliff-dwelling Anasazi, nor to the people who built the early pueblos even. The Navajos showed up here a good while after the Basketmakers quit this region."

"If you're sure of that, tell me where they took off to."

This was evidently something he wasn't able to answer. It undoubtedly griped him but he brushed it aside. "I'll tell you something else," he earnestly declared. "Over the centuries both the Basketmakers and their near kin the Pueblos received and amalgamated continual additions to their cultural inventory. Such improvements eventually as stone axes and pottery, the hard cradleboard, permanent housing and that marvelous weapon the bow and arrow—none of these luxuries had come to this country with them. They even learned to domesticate wild turkeys."

"What about the horse?"

"They knew nothing of horses. The Spaniards didn't set foot in America until two or three hundred years after the last of Basketmakers had completely disappeared. The term *Anasazi* in the Navajo use of it means simply 'ancient enemies,'" he assured me, "but why those old Basketmakers should have been considered enemies is completely up in the air. The two cultures, far as we know, never even came close to any confrontation. Indeed, how could this have been possible when the Navajos' arrival found this region up for grabs?"

"Do you reckon," I said, "if I had gotten here sooner . . ."

Jeff laughed. "Anyway, according to the best current advice on the subject, somewhere about two thousand years ago this primitive and extremely simple people lived scattered in pretty small groups over much of this region. In appearance and culture they've been likened to the Australian aborigines—not that our present Indians bear much resemblance. It might surprise you to learn I've been told a man can step back seven hundred years and more just rounding a bend in some of those draws and canyons. Kind of grips you, doesn't it? These ancient long-abandoned ruins, I'm told, are mostly found in sandstone country, tucked away in caves and plastered overhangs."

"I expect we can promise to show you a few. Don't know as you'll discover a great deal you'll want to cherish. Might even come up with one nobody's seen except for those usin' it. There's still a few hostiles runnin' loose and, hard though he tried, there are still a few scalawags Mossman an' company never got their hands on."

He peered around sharply. "You honestly believe—?"

"Wouldn't surprise me a heap if we run into some pretty hard cases. Not red ones though. You won't find many Indians around those ruins—live ones, I mean. They don't consider such places healthy. Too much chance of scarin' up a chindi."

"Spirits? You don't imagine they really *believe* in such foolishness?"

"You bet," I told him. "Never mind. You've got a forty-sixty chance of stumbling onto some ruin nobody yet has ever blundered into."

CHAPTER THREE

Having fixed my own grub times without count, I thought maybe offering my services as cook might take a little heat off my own situation so far as it applied to Hatcher and company. According about the middle of the afternoon I pushed a reluctant Gretchen into overtaking Fern where she rode with Jeff a broiling hundred yards ahead.

"How's the dust back there?" Jeff asked, swabbing a wipe across flushed cheeks.

"No worse than it is up here," I said. "What are you folks fixin' to do about a cook? I could patch up a meal if you can't do any better."

She kept whatever reaction she had under cover. "Turtle Jones has agreed to take over that department. Seems he spent last fall being roundup cook for Colonel Green's outfit."

"That's fine." I grinned. "Can't say I was ackshully lookin' forward to that sort of chore." After her brother rode off to rejoin Hatcher up ahead I said to Fern, "How long does Hatcher figure it's like to take to put Jeff where he can start his hunt?"

"He says he don't want to push these horses. That it most likely will take us five or six days."

I looked off through the smudge of heat and dust where the pack string plodded up a shallow draw. A couple of the crew were hoisting canvas water bags to put a bit of damp on their whistles. "You ever think to ask Harry what he hopes to get out of this?"

"Get out of it? You've already asked; we both heard what he said. What could he think to get beyond the fee he and Jeff agreed on?" Her stare seemed puzzled. "It isn't Harry you've got to watch. Why, Jeff thinks Hatcher is the luckiest find he could possibly have made!"

"Just what's he payin' Harry, if you don't mind sayin'?"

She looked at me intently, halfway shrugged and presently mentioned Hatcher was to get one hundred and fifty dollars a week to furnish crew and transport, locate a suitable spot for the dig and fetch all Jeff found back where we'd started from. Pretty good pay I was bound to agree, but someway it left me less than satisfied. I glanced at the dog ambling alongside Fern's mount with her tongue lolling out but still going strong and taking pleasure in this romp.

"And who picks up the supplies, the grub and what-not?"

"Harry picked them up under Jeff's instructions; Jeff and I paid for them. Look—" she said, "I don't see the point to this. What are you getting at?"

"Nothin' wrong with the deal. It all hinges on Hatcher. If you can take him at face value, if you're satisfied the feller's no more than he claims to be, this trip could be duck soup." I touched Gretchen up with a spurless heel, Fern scrambling after us.

"I told you Jeff trusts him, sees nothing in Fletcher and Clampas to bother him."

"But you went out of your way to pull me into—"

"That's right," she said with no attempt to duck around it. "I'm afraid of those two. I don't like their looks, can't see why Harry, if it was simply a matter of running into something we hadn't allowed for, couldn't have found—"

"Yeah. You told me. He obviously picked them figurin' if we ran into gunplay they'd be tough enough to earn whatever he's payin' them. Same notion you was fondlin' when you came after me." I considered her disgustedly. "What if Harry can't control them? Were they known to him beforehand?

An' what do you suppose'll happen if he can't? If he decides to pull out?"

"If you want to back out—"

"Get rid of that notion. I'm not backin' out. Just tryin' to make sure you understand where you're at in this business. That's a damn lonesome country Harry's takin' you into; you better go into it with both eyes open. Your brothers's a babe in the woods."

There was color in her cheeks, an angry sparkle in her glance. "You sound—"

"Never mind that. If Hatcher decides to pull out and leave you—"

"Leave us where?"

"In that wonderful place he's been talkin' about that no other paleface has ever set eyes on."

"We've got a contract with Harry. I don't see how he could pull out. The bank assured us—"

"If Hatcher's got other plans, that piece of paper won't stop him."

About an hour short of sundown Harry threw up a hand. Declared we'd gone far enough for the start of this journey and would make camp here where these mesquites and ironwoods would afford some protection should a wind come up and start belting through this sand.

It wasn't a bad place. Plenty of dead wood for the fires and a small creek gurgling over gray rocks between moss-covered banks. Ample room to set up the tents, one for Fern and the other fetched along as a cover for our supplies. He told Turtle Jones to get busy with the small fire and fixings, and the rest of the crew to get our stuff off the pack string. Fletcher he picked to take care of the horses and Clampas he posted atop a rock with a rifle. He seemed to know what he was doing.

I took Gretchen to the stream and let her have a small drink. I considered the scanty forage as I rubbed her down with a piece of gunnysacking, then limped over to the bags of grain we'd brought along for the horses and dumped a couple quarts of oats into a nosebag for her. I didn't bother with hobbles, knowing from long experience she wouldn't stray beyond reach of my call. They had the horses, likewise with nosebags, penned inside a hastily thrown up rope corral.

With no chuck wagon to work from you had to give Turtle Jones high marks for the potluck meal he put together this first night.

As Jeff remarked in the midst of our eating, "That chef we stole from the Waldorf-Astoria has more than lived up to his great reputation," and handsome Harry cried, "Stand up, boy, and take a deserved bow!"

"Aw, shucks," Jones muttered with his cheeks firing up, "ever'thing come outa cans but them biscuits. If I kin ever git organized I'll try to do better."

Most everyone sat around the fire that first evening singing old range songs to Alfredo the handyman's accompaniment on his mouth harp. Fern left Jeff to come and flop down beside me with her mop of roan hair, eyes brighter than the stars, that splatter of freckles across her nose hardly showing and denim-clad legs tucked snugly under her.

"Mighty well-behaved dog," I said, eyeing Flossie where she crouched nearby with her behind reared up, face on paws, glance fixed on me intently.

Fern laughed. "I think she likes you. Look—she wants to play! She almost never barks, she puts all her thoughts in body language."

"How'd you come to give her that name?"

"She's named after a girl I went to school with. She wasn't even weaned when I got her, just a pitiful stray I picked up off the streets. We had to feed her from a bottle. When she got old enough to eat from a pan, she insisted on me holding it while she lay stretched out across my lap. When finally I refused any longer to accommodate her she used to sprawl on the floor beside her pan—it was nearly a year before she'd eat standing up. See! She knows we're talking about her."

The dog rolled over on her back, watching me upside down, waggling her paws. "I don't think she'll let you but that's what she does when she wants her stomach rubbed."

I reached out a hand. Quick as a wink the dog ducked out from under it. "She's shy." Fern laughed. "Come on, Flossie. Time to go to bed."

We all turned in fairly early that night, myself finding sleep hard to come by, too many wild thoughts chasing through my head like a herd of spooked horses. Coyotes yapped back and forth across the moonlit distance. Crickets chirped and nighthawks swooped and between unrestful periods of dozing I tried to keep a weather eye on Clampas and Fletcher taking turn and turn about atop that twelve-foot flat-topped rock.

The night passed without untoward alarms or excursions. It was Jones beating a racket from his washtub with a ladle brought me out of my soogans while the only light in the solid dark came from the built-up breakfast fire. "Come an' git it!" he yelled.

By my figuring we had covered some thirty miles—perhaps a bit more than less—in that first day's travel toward an uncertain future. On this second day we did better. The horses' high spirits in the cool of that early morning and the exasperated shouts and cursing of the crew were not allowed to impede Hatcher's schedule and there was no lallygagging permitted on the trail.

During most of the morning Fern rode ahead with Harry and her brother and I'd had plenty of time to sort out my notions had I been able to put my mind to it. There was always the chance Jeff was right about Hatcher though I couldn't persuade myself that was likely. The man was too glib, too agreeable, too obliging in furthering Larrimore's views and aspirations.

About Fletcher and Clampas I had no doubts at all. Until Mossman's advent this state had been more than rife with their kind. Cut-and-run killers of every shade and description had all but taken over the towns; stages were stopped, often ransacked and burned, rustlers and horse thieves made ranchers' lives miserable. Claim jumping had become the biggest business you could find in the outback. Some of these rascals had become so slick that, as Burt Mossman had been heard to declare, it took one to know one.

Burt's boys, the Rangers he'd been picked to head and organize, could not afford to wear any mark of their calling. Arizona was a gun-governed country and its Rangers looked just like anybody else. Tough and enduring, hard-nosed survivors on call night and day, loners by necessity.

The sun grew hotter as the day wore along; you dared not rest a hand on any piece of metal. An egg would have fried anyplace it was dropped, but we had no eggs and we ate in the saddle, ignoring the customary stop for noon. "We don't have to push these broncs," Hatcher said, "but on the other hand we don't want to waste a lot of time. Steady riding will eat up the miles and put us in the next camp with something still left in case it has to be called for." His quick stabbing glance brushed across sweat-streaked faces. "Keep your minds on your business and be damn careful with that water."

It occurred to me to wonder where Harry imagined he was bound for but I didn't figure it behooved me to put in my gab in the face of his authority. Unless he got on to himself before we squandered tomorrow, the schedule he'd laid out was going to come up mighty short. It crossed my mind Larrimore might like a look at Inscription House, a ruin so named for the seventeenth-century date chiseled onto it by some forgotten Spaniard. Jeff, I reckoned, wouldn't come within miles of it.

Hatcher was being only prudent in warning the crew to conserve their water. But I thought those very words showed the man lacked considerable of being near as smart as young Larrimore esteemed him. Nothing but sheer ignorance could get a man killed of thirst around here. This was Basketmaker country; as Jeff delighted in mentioning, they had lived in this region for hundreds of years and they certainly hadn't thrived without water.

Toward the shank of the afternoon Jeff dropped back for a powwow. Seemed a bit embarrassed about announcing what he'd come for. "Get it off your chest," I said. "You must've come back here for somethin'."

"Well . . . doesn't it look like to you Harry's going the long way around?"

"How so?"

"Hadn't we ought to be heading a lot more to the east than he's taking us?"

"Why not ask him if you feel strong enough about it? Ain't he the one you're payin' to get you there? He's the man you said was on back-slappin' terms with these environs."

"But you said," Jeff protested, "you'd recently come through the place we're supposed to be heading for."

"Some fellers say a heap more'n their prayers. Direction he's goin', there's all sorts of red cliffs—"

"But not the ones I'd figured to be finding." He looked a mite grim about the edges of his mouth. "I might be what you call a tenderfoot," he said pretty harsh, "but by cripes I haven't yet lost all my marbles! If you won't tell me, would you advise my sister?" He was some het up, no two ways about it.

Lifting one of those skinny cigars from his pocket, I bit off an end and fired up.

"Wouldn't want me to cramp Harry's style now, would you?"

He slammed me a long look and suddenly,

40

spinning his mount, took off for the head of the line again.

Result of all this became immediately evident. A considerable commotion broke out up ahead. Dust churned as the whole file of horsebackers, pack string and all, stopped like they had run plumb into a brick wall. Angry voices sawed through the confusion. *"Where's that sonsabitchin' mule man!"* Hatcher shouted, and here he came with blood in his eye.

Pulling up so short his horse reared, snorting, right on top of me almost, his yell crashed out of a livid face. "What d'you think you're playing at, Corrigan! What'd you tell that goddam fool?"

"Seemed to think we'd got off our course, wanted me to confirm it." I smiled at him thinly. "Told him you was runnin' this outfit; if he had any beef he should take it to you."

The hot glare from those eyes showed him still a far piece from any kind of shape to be reasoned with. I thought it best to try anyhow. "Your contract," I said, "as I understand it, gives you authority to take this outfit in whatever direction you figure will best serve. So why not go on with it?"

"You trying to get me fired off this job?"

"*Can* he fire you?" I said to him soberly. "He's just one dude against the whole push of you. Wouldn't think he'd get much change out of that."

"Maybe not," Harry growled after rummaging through it. "Just the same, you keep your damn yap out of this," and he went pounding off in a great rise of dust.

No telling what he said to young Larrimore but evidently they managed to patch up their differences because not ten minutes later our whole line of travel bent off to the right.

CHAPTER FOUR

We camped late that night with the dark congealing round us and Jones in a temper, short of wood and with no water available save for what still sloshed in the bags on our saddles. Refried beans was heaviest item on the menu.

No sitting around the fire at this place, no grins or pranks. Mouth harps, singing and the usual big windies were conspicuous by their absence. Fern with Flossie went early to bed. Fletcher went up a palo verde with his rifle looking sour enough to curdle fresh milk and Clampas, similarly armed, went off someplace back of the rope holding down our remuda.

Nobody said one word in my direction, not even Jones showed a friendly face. With not the frailest notion what Hatcher might come up with as a suitable reprisal for giving in to Larrimore, I kept Gretchen handy and slept with a pistol under my hull.

We were up before sunrise and on our way within the hour, some of us half scalded with the heat Jones flung into that java. The sky turned pink and the landscape brightened and the sun shot up in all its glory smackdab into the horses' faces.

The country looked flat, stretching out long miles in its mildly undulant surface through its haze of brown dust.

Larrimore, despite any change he'd effected yesterday, appeared fidgety with visible worry lines about his stare. "Yes," Fern said when later she dropped back to ride beside me, "he was pretty upset. He had a terrible row with Hatcher when Harry threatened to quit and pull the crew out with him. I think what bothered him more than anything was having his faith in the man undermined. Jeff was banking heavily on Harry's ability to put him onto a real find."

"I expect they'll get over it. Hatcher's lettin' off steam; I don't reckon he'll quit. Not yet anyway."

"That," she said, eyeing me in some concern, "wasn't the impression I got from you yesterday."

"Just wanted you to consider the possibilities is all. I can't tell what he's up to; if it suited whatever's runnin' through his noggin he could leave you in a minute, but I shouldn't think he's anywhere near doin' it yet. And as for pullin' out with all hands, some of these boys might not see it his way. You can bet he won't leave before Jeff gets his dig started."

She looked a little reassured. "How big is this Chaco Canyon?" she asked.

"Pretty big. Some ten miles long and I'd guess about a mile wide between the walls. A heap of ruins in that space. Those old boys certainly built for the centuries. I've poked around in a couple—"

"Is there much there to find?"

"Depends what you're lookin' for. Probably find a few pots but I doubt they'd be old enough to interest Jeff. He wants to get back to the beginnings of these people. I'm afraid any relics he might come across there, except perhaps the buildings themselves, probably

44

wouldn't be things actually used by those Basketmakers—not the early ones. Best bet," I told her, "is to hunt them side canyons and gulches branchin' off it.

"All the towns—if you can call them that—along the Chaco itself were big places in their time. Most of them had several hundred rooms plus ceremonial chambers. Much like the pueblos bein' lived in today. Most of them—even those that haven't been looked over by folks in Jeff's line of work—have still had a mort of people prowlin' through them."

"Why would those gulches be less likely to be picked over?"

"Some of them ain't so easy to come onto, either deliberately hidden or screened by brush that's grown up through the ages. All the trees within ten miles of the Chaco were cut away and used up at different times by the builders. But get back in some of them tributary canyons and you're dealin' with buildings of sixty rooms and less."

I found her studying me curiously. "You sound as though you know as much about it as Harry."

"Can't speak for Hatcher. About all I personally know comes of observation. Anyone meanderin' over this desert learns to keep his eyes peeled. Same as Flossie," I told her, grinning down at her watchful sheepdog.

She said, "If Harry hasn't taken this job for what we're paying him, what do you suppose he's after?"

"Loot."

She looked considerably surprised. "Well . . . I know—I quite realize the relics Jeff hopes to find and identify would possibly be worth a little something to collectors, but . . ."

"Some people would put up a king's ransom for such things if they went back far enough in reasonably good condition and had nothing broken out of them. And the more rare the object the more they'll fork over. Looting's an enticing and highly profitable occupation for more people than you'd imagine."

"Now and again," she said like she was studying on it, "you use words few persons hereabouts have ever bumped into."

"Yeah," I said. "It's a damn bad habit I've found hard to get shut of."

That night we camped alongside an arroyo where Hatcher went down into an apparently dry wash with a short-handled shovel he got out of the camp gear. He didn't have to dig for more than five minutes hardly before the hole began filling with water. Jeff allowed we'd be more comfortable camping down in that wash but Hatcher knew better. "A man can mighty quick wake up drowned doing that around here. You get a storm up in the mountains you've got ten-twelve foot of water in this wash."

While three of the crew and Fletcher was getting the loads off the pack string the other two hands began fetching the saddle mounts down for a drink. I dumped my water bag into my hat and held it while Gretchen cooled her insides, then anchored her to grounded reins and went over and put up the tent for Fern. Jones broke up a couple creosote bushes and got his fire started and Clampas with rifle found him a station on the lip of the arroyo, Hatcher going across to have a few words with him.

I pitched in to help water the pack string while somebody else busied himself setting up the rope corral and pouring oats into nosebags to hang on the horses. I rubbed Gretchen down with my piece of gunnysack and wiped out her nostrils. By that time Turtle Jones had a good bed of coals and was dexterously throwing together our supper which, praise be, tonight featured no refried beans, Alfredo the handyman scouting up wood.

On Hatcher's advice we went early to bed and once more with a pistol stashed ready for use I kept Gretchen by me in case of quick need. No breeze sprang up to whine through the straggle of wind-bent trees along the arroyo's rim where Clampas stood with his rifle. We'd have a late moon tonight and, by the look of things, a hot day tomorrow which most likely was the reason Hatcher aimed to be moving ahead of daylight. Being short on sleep I drifted off almost at once.

Something jolted me awake. Grabbing up my six-shooter I peered through the dregs of the moon's fitful glow to find Gretchen's whiskers not three inches from my cheek. Throwing off my cover I came onto an elbow. There was some kind of hubbub boiling up beyond the penned stock, punctuated by horse sounds and angry voices. Gretchen, sidling closer, softly blew out her breath. Fletcher's furious yell sailed through the racket.

"That goddam mule man! Told you to git rid of him! Prob'ly turned them critters loose a-purpose!"

I got out of my soogans, put a hand out to Gretchen.

Jeff came shoving out of the shadows. "What's the rumpus?" Beyond him Jones was building up his fire. Catching up Gretchen's reins I headed for the corral and the group standing around that motionless huddle on the ground.

"What's happened?" Jeff demanded, singling out Hatcher.

"We're short one man and two of the broncs."

"Who is it?" Larrimore wanted to know.

"Ned Benson."

"Is he hurt?"

Fletcher's sarcastic growl said, "Why would he hurt? Hell, he's never been happier!"

"He's dead," Hatcher said. "Been walloped over the head."

I said, "How'd those broncs get loose from the corral?"

"You tell us," Fletcher snarled, starting toward me.

Hatcher thrust him back, hard eyes digging into me. "You got anything to say?"

Two of the boys stepped aside to let Fern through. "Brice had nothing to do with this. You had Clampas on guard—didn't he hear anything?"

Hatcher's stare swiveled to Clampas. "Well?"

"Nary a thing," Clampas told us. "Whoever done this must've moved on bare feet."

"Maybe you fell asleep," Fern said, and Clampas snorted. "Whoever done this was Injun quiet."

Jeff's face looked troubled. Hatcher looked worried, near as I could make out in that uncertain light. I said, "What makes you think two horses are missing?"

"They're missin' all right. Soon's I spotted Benson I slipped in there an' made a count," Fletcher grumbled. Fern and Jeff exchanged a quick look. I said, "If someone was trying to make trouble for us, why stop with two horses? Why not grab all of them?"

Hatcher nodded. "Good point. Couple of Navajos probably snuk up on us someway."

"Come an' git it!" Jones called.

He'd beat up some biscuits and what he gave us to go with them was refried beans.

Harry told off a couple hands to bury Benson, made sure all water bags were filled and hustled us out of that place just as the sky was beginning to turn gray. He and Jones had gone through the supplies and none of the foodstuffs appeared to be missing, but the loss of Benson—not to mention two horses—had put a damper on our spirits. It was a pretty subdued outfit that got under way that morning.

Clampas dropped back to ride alongside me, but had nothing to offer in the way of conversation. After a couple of hours Hatcher came back and motioned Clampas to move on ahead. "This Chaco," he asked me. "How much farther do you reckon it to be?"

"Another couple days, if we push them a mite, ought to fetch us in sight of the south gap, I reckon. Thought you knew all about that canyon."

Harry's face put on a sort of rueful scowl. "Tell you the truth I ain't never been near it. There's red rocks lots of places. I was figuring, long as he wouldn't know the difference, to take him up into them Lukachukai Mountains. Figured he could dig there good as anyplace." He hawked up some phlegm and spit it off to the side. "How do you look at that business last night? Think it was Indians?"

"What about Fletcher? Heard him tryin' to lay it onto me. He wouldn't think no more about killin' a man than he would about findin' worms in his biscuits."

"Keep away from him," Hatcher grunted. "On pretty short notice I had to take what I could get." He kept looking into the swirl of heat haze ahead of where Clampas, lounging in the saddle, was riding point. "Country's changin'," he said. "Bunch grass and grama. Lot of rocks croppin' up—ain't none of them red though. You been through here before?"

"Don't rightly remember."

"Didn't somebody say your old man run a tradin' post?"

"He runs the post at Half Step."

"Doin' pretty good, is he?"

"Gettin' by, I reckon."

"You in that business?"

"Guess I'm too fiddle-footed. Too much settin' around. Too quiet."

"How come," he asked, "you don't ride a horse?"

"I find this mule more dependable. She don't spook so easy, for one thing."

Hatcher's stare wheeled around. "Man could get lost damn easy round here. Mile after mile it all looks alike. Can't see how them Basketmakers stood it. Dry as a brick horn."

"Expect it didn't used to look like this. Don't hardly ever rain here no more."

There was about Harry this morning a suggestion of something stewing in his craw which he wanted to get up but was making rough work of. Two–three times he'd cleared his throat, the gloom in his stare wandering over my face while he chewed on his lip with unaccustomed indecision.

Something hauled my thoughts away from him. Scrinching my eyes, trying to cut through the pack-string dust up ahead, I said, "Company comin'."

It jerked Hatcher's head up. We could both see them now. Jeff coming back with two other horsemen.

"Navajos!" Hatcher grunted, loosening the pistol in its housing on his hip.

When they came up, swinging their horses to ride alongside us, the older Indian, wrinkled of face and gray of hair, was energetically puffing one of Larrimore's thin cigars with every evidence of relish. Jeff with a glance at Hatcher said, "They want to know what we're doing here."

Harry looked them over and with hand on gun butt contemptuously spat. The younger Navajo's eyes turned hateful. I could see pretty quick this could get a little touchy. "We're huntin' old pots from the time of the Anasazi," I told the old man.

"I think you better leave," he answered.

53

"This land," he said with a hand taking in everything in sight, "belongs to the People."

"Since when?" Hatcher challenged.

"Many years—"

"Soldiers say different."

Both Indians took a long look about. The older man smiled. "No soldiers here," he announced with satisfaction. "You go."

Hatcher smiled, too. A nasty thin-lipped grimace; and there was Clampas with his rifle coming down the line to join us. "This man," I said, putting a hand out toward Jeff, "is a friend to the People from a great white man's school far away. He'd like to take back some things—"

"All white men take. Too much take!" the younger Navajo growled. "All time take!"

We had all come to a stop in the sort of confrontation that could bode no good for anyone. Something had to be done before a bad situation piled up a worse hereafter. Clearing my throat I said to the old one, "This teacher," with a nod of the head at Larrimore, "is tryin' to find the Chaco. He wants to tell the men at his school of all the wonderful things built there by the people who left this land for the Navajos."

Those Indian faces didn't offer much encouragement. Cold sweat came out along the back of my neck. I waved Clampas back. "So if you'd agree," I said, "to act as scouts for this outfit and show us the fastest, most direct way to get there—"

"What you give?" Greedy interest was all over that young buck; and Jeff, catching on, held out his watch to the older one, who gravely accepted it, holding it up to an ear, smiling at the sound it made. The other Indian spurned such baubles. "You give tobacco? Blue stones? You give whiskey?"

I looked at him sternly. "Whiskey bring soldiers. We give tobacco. Frijoles. A tall hat for each of you."

"Give me a chew of tobacco now," the younger one demanded.

I reached into my pocket and handed him my plug, from which he took a great bite and threw the rest in the dust. "You give gun!"

There was naked envy in the way he was staring at the Sharps across Clampas's saddlebow. "No guns," I said, and he glared at me malevolently. "You already have a gun," I told him, pointing to the Henry rifle on his saddle.

"That gun no good." He thrust out a hand toward Clampas. "Give me that one!"

"Where do you want it?" Clampas growled without expression.

"Maybe so," the fellow said, grinning, "some Indian kill you."

"Have at it," Clampas invited, and elevated his Sharps to bear on the man at point-blank range.

CHAPTER FIVE

White about the mouth Jeff said, "Put that down. We don't shoot people at a friendly powwow, nor while we're crossing Navajo land."

Clampas for a moment appeared to be of two minds. Before things got out of hand, Harry kneed his own horse sufficiently forward to blank out the threat. The old man, seeming unaware of the danger and smiling sadly at Larrimore, finally spoke. "What you say is good. Since I was no higher than your dog the white man has brought us nothing but trouble. I have not forgotten when bluecoat soldiers took the People away, but your heart is good." Still considering Jeff he sat quietly a moment, then abruptly said, "That we may live at peace I will take you to the Chaco."

The two Indians rode with Larrimore past the stopped pack string and forward to the head of the line. Harry released pent breath and looked at me with a shudder. "A near thing, that." His darkening glance found Clampas. "Stay away from that fellow." The laden pack string began to move, but in a new direction, still east but more southerly. Clampas rasped a fist across flushed cheeks. "We'll have to watch that buck," he told Hatcher. "We ain't outa this yet by a long shot."

It was obvious Harry agreed. "Have to post more guards at night. Long as they're with us. Old man's all right, but that younger one might be brash enough to try and stampede the whole string."

"Could fix him up with a accident mebbe."

Harry gave him a sharp look. "Don't even think of it. That old duffer looks like to me he might have a bigger than average say hereabouts—in Chaco too for all we know."

"You're probably right," I said. "We sure don't want to fetch the whole tribe down on us. You heard what he said about white men and trouble. He's peaceable now; we ought to do our best to keep him that way."

Clampas slapped the butt of his Sharps

disgustedly. "Pamperin' them bastards won't buy you nothin'. Put it into their heads you kin be pushed around an' by Gawd you'll *git* pushed! If you wanta git along with'em you got to take a firm stand."

That night we made another dry camp.

Wood—even cowflops—was in short supply but Jeff, no doubt as concession to our red friends, ordered Jones to spread himself and we had the best meal we'd been served in six nights. Jerked beef cut up in some kind of white gravy, spuds baked in the ashes with their jackets on, hot buttered biscuits and coffee strong enough to stand without a cup. And canned peaches to round things off.

True to what they'd been offered, Jeff gave each Indian a black uncreased Stetson, a small sack of dried beans, and tobacco. The chewing sort. In addition to this largess the older man was ceremoniously presented with a good round dozen of Larrimore's thin cigars.

Before the rest of us turned in, Harry arranged for three shifts of men armed with rifles to patrol the perimeters and make sure none of the horses managed to get themselves lost. This possibly wasn't necessary but, reminded of the loss we'd already taken and a pair of Indians right in our midst, I couldn't blame Harry for trying to play safe. He had to see that Jeff remembered that a man without a horse in this kind of country was in mighty sorry shape.

It looked like being another hard night. I couldn't rid my head of the many disquieting notions continuing to churn up unwanted activity. Generally I could put such things out of mind but certain faces in this outfit continued to plague me, not the least of which was Fern's.

I recalled how before the start of this jaunt I'd considered her a plain damn nuisance, arrogant and headstrong and like to be a pain in the ass insisting on having a part in this deal. Since then I'd learned she could grow on a man, no fool at all but a girl with real pluck and a heap more sense in a practical way than that dreamy-eyed Jeff with his talk of dead Indians and artifacts nobody else had dug up.

Thoughts of Hatcher and his deadly companions continued to rile and disturb me. For all the airs he put on, his talking talents and confident authority, it appeared to me dubious that if push came to shove he'd be at all able to control that pair.

First thing I'd done when we'd quit for the day was to take care of Gretchen and put up Fern's tent. "Stay away from those Navajos," I told her, but all I'd got out of that was an odd look and laughter. She said, "That old man is no scalp-hunting redskin." A mischievous light danced round in her stare. "He told me his name—Johnny Two-Feathers. Isn't that quaint? The other one's Hosteen Joe—"

"It's that other one we got to watch out for."

"Johnny'll keep him in line. He's pretty well educated by local standards. Brought up by the Jesuits in mission schools, first in Tubac and again at Tucson; even knows a few words in Latin! Don't you hate to think of a man that old having to sleep on the ground?"

"Fern," I said, "he's been doing it all his life."

"You know what he calls you? 'Man-on-a-Mule.'" Her laugh tinkled again like silver bells in the sunset. "He calls Jeff 'Young Man Who Hunts Old Ones.'"

He had certainly made an impression on Fern—a notion I wasn't at all sure I cared for.

Just as I was finally about to drop off,

young Jeff came over and squatted down for a chat. "You know," he said, "I believe I've caught up with the bee in Harry's bonnet. I heard him asking old Johnny about beads—"

"May be fixin' to do a little trading on the side," I told him. "Better get some sleep."

Jeff's mention of beads in connection with Harry became one more notion I didn't like the look of. But nothing happened in the night and once again we got off to an extra early start with old Johnny up there at the front of the line and Hosteen Joe and his surly scowls noplace in sight.

Hatcher dropped back and I brought this up. "I dunno," Harry said. "He's out there ahead of us someplace, making sure—according to Johnny—we don't run into trouble. Between you and me and the gatepost he's more like to stir it up and kick the lid off if he can."

Refried beans juned around in my stomach. Dust devils spun across the empty flats and heat waves shimmered and danced in the distance. Noon came and went without rest and no edibles, with the gritty shadow shapes of men and horses drearily toiling in dust-choked silence beside us.

As the afternoon wore on, the gray scraps

of clay hills filled with shale began to lift and crawl with interminable monotony across the trackless landscape. There was no sign at all of the missing Joe, nor did he turn up for supper when we stopped at a seep to pitch camp for the night.

Harry growled at me bodingly, "That son-ofabitch is up to something!"

But the night was got through without alarm or apparent mishap. For breakfast we had corn bread and another dose of refried beans. Plus some of Jones's Arbuckle. No one had much to say. We got away bright and early, Johnny Two-Feathers riding again with Fern at the front of the outfit, Clampas and Fletch flanking their progress about a hundred yards out.

The morning breeze wafting across that seared and blackened vista ghosted away within the hour and the molten disk of the rising sun began to get in its licks. Hatcher, swinging his mount in alongside Gretchen, gave me a brief unjoyous grin. "Don't blame them basket-makin' aborigines for getting the hell out of this place! Enough to cramp rats!" he growled, sleeving his face.

"Probably better when those cliff towns were buildin'. Expect they had more rain; Chaco was likely runnin' bank to bank. I remember Jeff saying they did quite a bit of farming down on the flats."

"What kind of boodle you reckon he's really after?"

I flipped him a look. "You know what he's here for. No secret about it; he's hopin' to unearth the Anasazi's beginnings and dig up enough evidence to prove—"

"You ain't swallerin' that hogwash, are you?"

"What's your idea?"

"I think he's after turquoise. Why else would his sister rope *you* into this?" Harry peered at me sharply as if to see how I was taking it. "Your old man runs a trading post. Among these redskins, from what I've seen, there's a big demand for them blue stones!" He let the silence stretch out, squirming round for a better look at my face. "Hell, some of them bucks would trade their women off for'em! I been told," he said, watching, "it's been a prime source of feuding down through the ages—oldest gemstone known."

"Even so," I told him, "what you're thinkin' don't make a heap of sense. Jeff's an academic, a professor of anthropology. His notions in that field look pretty reasonable, I'd say. The man is after kudos, the kind of acceptance and undoubted publicity he could get overnight if he's able to dig up the kind of factual evidence no one has managed to turn up before. He ain't the first of his kind to put a dig on out here, you know. There've been others—the Wetherills, for instance."

Hatcher wasn't convinced. "Maybe. But you take it from me there's something besides old pots drivin' that dude. I've got a hunch he's stumbled onto something. Big an' blue and buried in that canyon!"

CHAPTER SIX

The next day was Sunday.

The night before, while I was putting Fern's tent up, old Johnny had sought me out to say he would soon be released from his obligation, that we should see the red cliffs before another night. This knowledge trickling through the camp had set up a certain amount of excitement, put a new look on the faces of our outfit.

To go with our breakfast coffee Jones gave us nothing but yesterday's biscuits. Harry paid no mind to the grumbling, as anxious to get moving as Jeff was himself. By six o'clock we were well on our way, myself as usual still riding drag with Fletcher and Clampas out several hundred yards ahead of the pack string.

Fern came back to swap a few words with me. I said, "Who had the ordering of grub for this outfit?"

"That was Harry's department. In his behalf I'll have to point out we've a better variety than Jones has dished up. There's quite a bit of tinned beef but Jones is afraid of it with all this heat. The cans aren't bulged; I believe it's all right." The roan mop of her hair was windblown and tousled. "What were you and Harry so earnest about yesterday?"

"He's got it into his head all this talk about Basketmakers is just so much crap, that your brother's after turquoise—"

"Turquoise!" she cried, eyes locked on mine widely. "Where did he pick up that silly notion?"

"He's been workin' on it. Only thing that makes sense to gents of Hatcher's persuasion is a whopping pile of dollars and the quickest way to get them. He simply can't believe two dudes from Chicago would come all this way just to dig up a bunch of old pots and such."

She bit her lip, looked worried. "That's

ridiculous! Exasperating!" The blue-green eyes intently searching my face became anxious. "You don't believe that, do you? I swear it isn't true—for years Jeff has believed these earliest Basketmakers came to this region thousands of years before his colleagues can be brought to admit . . . he's been trying to get back far enough to prove it. This is something he feels very strongly about. If he can only dig up—"

"Yes." I nodded. "I'll go along with that."

She said in a burst of anger, "This idea of Hatcher's is utterly untrue! Oh—I'm afraid this is going to make trouble, Brice. If that notion gets around it could wreck this dig before it even gets started! I'm going to send Jeff back to talk with you."

Jeff looked flushed, and angry too, when some half hour later he swung his horse in beside me. "Fern's told me about Hatcher. I've just been talking to him; wasted breath!" he said bitterly. "The man's impossible! Just sits there and grins at everything I tell him!"

"That figures. Only thing he wants to hear about is profit. Did he threaten you again with taking the crew out of here?"

Jeff shook his head irritably. "No, he made me a proposition. The fellow's preposterous!"

"What kind of proposition?"

"The man's a mental case! Says he knows of a ready market that will pay big money for any turquoise we come onto, that if we find any gem-grade rough or mounted spiderweb we could make a real killing. He proposes we split, him and me, fifty-fifty. I reminded him again I wasn't looking for turquoise, that what he suggested was completely unethical. 'Who's talking about ethics?' he sneered. 'You better have your head looked at. I'm telling you this could be a goddam bonanza!'"

The look on his face was furious. "I tried to tell him it wasn't likely we'd come up with hardly more than a cupful of extremely old and crudely cut beads, and that whatever we found was going back to the university."

I said, "How did that strike him?"

"He just laughed. 'All right,' he said, 'you go dig up your pots and *I'll* hunt the turquoise and I'll be claiming every chunk that's found.' I was so mad I could hardly talk. 'Over my dead body!' I told him, and got another of those pitying grins. 'Wouldn't be surprised,' he said, 'if that could be arranged.' "

We looked at each other through an uncomfortable quiet. Heat writhed above the gray shale-covered ground and shimmered between the distant worn-down bluffs. We set off after the others.

"You'll be knowin', of course, you're not the first to come in here?"

"Yes." Larrimore nodded. "Simpson came here in '49, Jackson in '77. There were Hyde's expeditions of '96 and 1901. Artifacts were found; but what they uncovered, while extremely interesting, didn't even approach the beginnings of these people. What they took out was relatively modern, Basketmaker. Three and Pueblo stuff. There's got to be more underneath—that's why I came out here. If there's to be any proof of the dream I've been coddling it's got to be right in this area someplace."

He gave me an anguished, frustrated look. "What are we going to do?"

"Just now, nothing." I shook my head much as he had done. "Right now, if he's got the crew with him, we're crouched between a rock and a hard place. I don't believe more than three of those boys will side with him. I think we'll have Jones and maybe Alfredo.

But if it comes to a scrap, that's pretty rough odds. He's going to have Clampas and Fletcher for sure."

Jeff's gone-white face was filled with despair. I peered off across the scarps of those shimmering bluffs and, twisting, swung my glance to where the blue and wavering peak of a mountain thrust above the trembling haze. Jeff abruptly caught hold of my arm. "Look!" he cried, pointing—"isn't that the Chaco?"

I nodded. "The south gap. But it isn't where you're staring. What you're seeing's a mirage. Take a glance at your sister and that old man. You don't see them turning. They're goin' straight on."

Jeff sank back in his saddle. "What if I order—"

"You're not in a position right now to order anything. If Harry's passed the word, and you can bet he has, the greed he's built up in that pair of gunslingers could get you killed at the first sign of trouble. Leave it alone. I want to think about this."

The broiling hours dragged on. The sun sagged into its downhill slide. A little breeze sprang up, too hot to afford relief. When our shadows began to drop behind us the

Navajo, riding with Fern perhaps a quarter of a mile ahead, pulled his piebald pony to a stop with lifted arm. The whole line stopped. A mumble of voices reached us in a faint jumbled sound.

Jeff cried, "What are they talking about? Why have they stopped?"

"Let's go find out." I tightened my legs against Gretchen's ribs and pushed her into a trot, Jeff's mount following. Harry, Fletcher, the old man and Fern had all dismounted, the first pair staring like they couldn't believe it into a huddle of blasted rocks where a seep formed a pool of unexpected water. Fletcher scrubbed a fist across beard-stubbled cheeks. "Heap good water," Johnny Two-Feathers said. And Harry with a jerked-up glance at the sky slammed his hat on the ground. "We're campin' right here—we've rode far enough!"

No one felt inclined to argue with that. Alfredo got an armful of sticks and Turtle Jones began to build up a fire while a rope was stretched round the pack string and the crew began peeling off loads and saddles. In almost no time at all Jones was treating us to refried beans.

It was crowding six in lengthening shadows by the time tin cups and pans clattered into the washtub and those who cared for it began to light up. We were in a locality of old rocks and outcrops with night closing in and no prospects showing for a better tomorrow. Fletcher and Clampas with instructions from Hatcher went grumblingly away to take up stations with their sour looks and rifles; and it was at this moment, taking a final survey of our unenviable situation, that I saw Fern with Flossie making her way in my direction.

Hatcher's sharp stare had discovered this, too.

The grin fell off his face as the dog with lifted hackles, growling softly, bared her teeth. "You better keep that bitch in hand," he said, ugly, stopping in his tracks to stand and glower in my direction. Fern grabbed the dog's collar and Hatcher straightened up to send a scathing glance across her face before turning the full weight of his inspection on me.

"Things have taken a change in this setup. I can see you've been told," he chucked at me with a laugh. "From here on out, those who ain't with me are in line for bad trouble," and he went stamping off, muttering under his breath.

Gretchen waggled her ears and hee-hawed

like a rust-clogged pump rod. Hatcher half turned like he was minded to come back but presently went off without further remark.

Fern sank down, legs folding under her, with an audible sigh. "Jeff's going about with the look of a zombie."

"He's come too far to give it all up now."

"But what can we *do?* "He won't deal with Hatcher." There was a tremor in her voice. "He's just about lost all heart for this dig."

I had no doubt Hatcher'd meant what he said. He figured he'd got hold of his life's best chance and was going to stay with it come hell or high water. No use kidding ourselves about that.

"Maybe things'll look better in the morning." I put a hand on her shoulder and gave it a squeeze. She got wearily up with an attempt at a smile that came off so stricken I made an extra effort to promote a cheerful outlook, but what was there to say remembering Hatcher's ultimatum? I could probably get the drop on him, but with Clampas and Fletcher with the camp spread out under the snouts of their rifles, such a move would be worse than not doing anything. To effectively improve this situation at all, those two hard cases had to be near enough to Harry to hold all three at a decided disadvantage.

I watched her move toward the tent, Flossie ambling along beside her.

She'd made it apparent she was neither meek nor biddable. She might not be any beauty but I had learned she was a girl with a good bit of bottom, in the main optimistically good-humored and not one to find relish in a jaundiced view of things. A down-to-earth sort of person . . .

I hauled myself up with a muttered oath. This was not a time for that kind of thinking. My sort of drifting held no place for a woman and nobody knew this with more conviction than myself. If she and Jeff were to have any chance of wresting the whip out of Hatcher's hands, it behooved me to do something pretty damn quick.

CHAPTER SEVEN

Daybreak found us mounted and moving. By all the signs and signal smokes the next camp should place us in Chaco Canyon. I'd done a mort of thinking without latching on to the faintest glimmer of how to disabuse Harry of the notion he was boss. The fellow was much too cagey to be taken unawares or let himself be lured beyond reach of those gunslingers' rifles. Catching him off balance was going to take some doing.

The molten arc of the sky showed not the ghost of a cloud. The sun crashed down with insensate fury and all about us appeared not to have known a touch of moisture since the Anasazi vanished. If other springs existed in this burned black flat, no one but Navajos knew of their location. If this drought-ridden country had any charm we had yet to discover it, a grim and empty place steeped in the stillness of the centuries. Burning sands and swirling dust storms, a hard land to picture as ever having been any different, yet it surely had; no people could have settled and flourished for hundreds of years in such desolation.

I was in better case than most of our outfit for I had crossed this waste before. Had actually encountered a few of these ruins Jeff and his sister had come to investigate and drearily discerned how little could be hoped from digging ground already disturbed. To provide Jeff's theories any chance of proof, he had to have ground untrod through intervening ages. No easy chore, though I reckoned it possible if we could find some solution to Hatcher's threats.

There was little to be gained by openly

opposing him. Any such attempt must be a last-ditch risk, for he was obviously prepared for ruthlessly crushing any action we might launch. Any turning of the tables called for guile and much patience.

Needing to make Jeff understand this, I sent Gretchen forward. But Harry, catching this maneuver, came up at a brisk trot, forcing his horse in between Fern and Larrimore with a nasty grin. Ignoring him I went on to pull up beside Fletcher, hoping to start a bit of counterirritation. "Has Hatcher mentioned his latest scheme?"

"Fletcher's look crawled over me morosely. "Keep away," he growled. "I got nothin' to say to you," and shifted his rifle.

"The man's told Larrimore he's claiming any turquoise we happen to find. I imagine what he has in mind is beads or nuggets; you can generally find a few around any old ruin. Just wonderin' if he was intending to share with you boys."

Before the fellow had time to digest this or show enough expression to afford me any lead, Hatcher loped up with an oily smile. "Won't do you no good trying your blarney on Fletch. Or anybody else. All my boys are in on this bonanza. Don't let me catch you suckin' up to'em again."

75

Turning away with a shrug I felt his hard look following. "If you want to start trouble," he called after me, "just stir up them dudes and you'll get yourself a bellyful."

The heat-blasted bluffs got closer and rougher as the morning dragged along. By this time, blue hazed in the distance, you could see where the south gap cut into the canyon and guess at the rubble that lay all around it. I was presently surprised, staring through the lifted dust, to find our old Navajo riding back in my direction. "How!" he hailed, swinging in beside me with a lifted hand. "Pretty soon I go."

"Thought maybe you were figurin' to throw in with us."

A faintly humorous glint briefly touched his glance. "White man's troubles like white man's whiskey. No good for Navajo. I got sheep to look after."

"You on your way?"

"Plenty soon. When you come to Chaco." He eyed me a moment. "You got message?"

"Heap smart Indian," I agreed with a grin. "Tell missy to keep her tongue between teeth. And tell her that goes double for her brother."

Watching his paint horse go loping back

to where Jeff and Fern rode at the head of the line, I wasn't at all hopeful he'd be allowed any private conversation. I saw Clampas gesture, saw Hatcher wheel and take a long crusty look. But contrary to my assumption, he sank back in the saddle and continued whatever he was laying on Clampas.

If only those dudes would take my words to heart I might have time enough to cobble together some means of forcing Hatcher to leave them alone, for it had to be Fern they'd level their spite at. It would be me they'd want to be rid of but might figure to keep me in line through the girl.

I kept cudgeling my brain without hitting on a notion that wasn't loaded with dire consequence should I fail to bring it off. That smart dog, Flossie, was sticking close to her mistress. The Navajo had left them to ride out a ways ahead, leaving the rest strung out behind; and Harry, abruptly beckoning Fletcher, turned his mount and swung toward me, the pair of them bracketing Gretchen.

Hatcher said belligerently, "So's you know where you stand in this, mister, I'm telling you now to stay away from my boys. You're not goin' to change'em, they're all in this with me. You make any trouble you're going to get hurt—*bad* hurt. Savvy?"

I forced a false admiration into my look. "I can see you don't miss much."

"You better believe it! I've got the whip hand and I intend to hang on to it. First wrong move outa you will be your last—just remember it."

With a final hard stare he wheeled away.

Fletcher, bending toward me, thrust out a hand, a jeering derision taking hold of his face. "Fork over that rifle an' don't give me no back chat." Hatcher had stopped and was watching intently. I pulled the Remington from its scabbard and held it toward him, butt forward. "You're learnin'," he chuckled, and galloped off after Harry.

Hatcher ordered camp pitched in the south gap entrance to the canyon. Jeff hadn't toted a rifle, nor had Alfredo or Jeff's sister, but Clampas had lifted Jones's artillery. I was surprised they hadn't taken my pistol. Hatcher probably figured, now that he'd spiked any attempt at sniping, to extract it later.

The Navajo departed with several more of Jeff's skinny cigars, and the crew got busy unloading the pack string while I tended to

Gretchen and put up Fern's tent. "Pin your faith on patience and don't start anything," I muttered as she ducked inside it.

Alfredo with sticks he had fetched from our last camp built up a small fire while the cook, with several tins stacked beside him, began beating up dough to put into his Dutch oven. I'd have hunted up more wood but there obviously wasn't any. What the Anasazi hadn't taken to put into roofs and ceilings the Pueblo builders had completely exhausted.

For supper, in addition to hot biscuits and lick, Jones had provided corned beef in abundance, saying he'd just come onto it and hoped we appreciated the effort. Nobody else said anything but all took copious helpings. When we had finished and dropped our pans and eating tools into Jones's tub, Harry asked Jeff where he was aiming to start his dig.

When Larrimore shrugged without answering, I took it on myself to say, "Not far from where we stand right now, just inside those walls, you'll see what's left of Una Vida. Lots of adders, rattlesnakes and gophers, but without an extensive dig I doubt if you'll be happy with anything you'll get. It's not one of the larger pueblos and there's not much left. I did pick up a handful of beads which," I added with a quick glance at Harry, "my old man managed to sell at considerable profit."

All that got from Hatcher was a grin. But Fletcher and a couple of the crew went off to try their luck. Harry said with curled lip, "Penny-ante stuff. Someplace hereabouts there's a big cache of stones that ain't never turned up—a whole goddam wagonful! That's what I'm aiming to get my hooks on. That or what Geoffrey here is goin' to find for me."

The gloat in his voice got under Fern's skin and the hot look she gave him would have withered an oak post, but Harry took it in stride with a satisfied chuckle. "Careful there, honey, you'll be poppin' a gasket." He rubbed a look across me. "Your old man trades in turquoise, don't he?"

"Expect he does when there's any call for it."

He dug in a pocket and tossed me a chunk about the size of a walnut. "How's that look to you?"

"I'm no expert."

"You must have seen enough to have some idea. Come on, be a sport. Fair, average, good or gem grade?"

I tossed it back. "About average."

Hatcher snorted. "That assayer at Ajo called it gem grade." His stare winnowed down to bright shining slits. "That's no way to get yourself cherished. Try playing along on my side of the fence an' you'll have a good chance of putting money in the bank."

I put in my glance a rapt admiration that drew a twinkle from Fern when I told him rueful-like, "With your flair and style you ought to own the bank by this time."

He kept the grin on his face but there was nothing to comfort in the cut of that stare. "Always the joker," he threw back at me smoothly. "When I drive that wagonload over to Half Step, your old man better figure to buy gem grade."

The sun was beginning to turn the sky pink all along the east flank of the little still left of Una Vida time we got through with breakfast next morning. Harry appeared bushy tailed and, at least on the surface, his old hearty self when "Well, Jeff," he said, "what's the program today? You aim to clear some of the rubble away from this site or try someplace else?"

"I believe the sensible way to tackle this

would be to have a good look at what's available first of all."

"You mean explore the whole canyon?"

Jeff nodded. To me he said, "You're the only one of us that's been here before, Brice. How many ruins are there?"

"Hell—I dunno. Ain't too much left of a lot of them. As I understand it these places were towns. Inside the canyon there probably ain't over five or six that look worth botherin' with and I expect every one of them has been pretty well pawed over."

Jeff said, "The two largest, I believe, are Pueblo Bonito and Chetro Ketl that Simpson examined in forty-nine. Hyde, too, did quite a bit of work at Pueblo Bonito just a few years ago I'm told. I'm not familiar with Wetherill's work or Putnam's, but Wetherill I think had a trading post somewhere in this area. Very likely he went over the best of these sites.

"I realize, of course, there may be more to uncover even in towns like Pueblo Bonito, but my time is limited. I'd probably do better tackling one of these sites like this one right here that appears too negligible to hold any interest."

"Let's get at it then," Harry grunted, rolling up his sleeves.

"I think I'd rather look at the rest first." He turned to me. "Wouldn't take over five or six days to see the lot, would it?"

"If it's just ridin' through without dawdlin' you can cover the whole canyon by nightfall."

"Will I see any cliff dwellings?"

"I can't recall any inside the canyon. There's places where the cliff walls are pretty well broken down with gulches leading off. Could be something back in there maybe."

"The point is," Jeff said in a thoughtful voice, "these pueblo towns mostly date back not more than seven hundred years. The earliest evidence of Basketmakers we know anything about—and precious little at that—indicate they were in this vicinity at least two thousand years ago. That's the period I'd like to put my dig in."

Hatcher said, glancing around, "Let's get the pack string loaded and be on our way."

During the next couple of hours it became fairly evident he had no intention of allowing private conversation between the Larrimores and me. He had them segregated up at the front with Clampas cozily riding between them, while keeping Fletcher and myself accompanying him behind the pack string and crew as the best way to thwart any trouble we might attempt to kick up.

He mightn't be smart but he could be plenty cunning when he put his mind to it.

We passed quite a number of ruins without pausing. Several textbooks had been published, mainly based on the investigations of earlier expeditions and the work of persons such as Wetherill and Putnam who, whatever they may have found, hardly did much more than scratch the surface. Along the eastern seaboard it seemed there were quite a number of people who wanted to know more about such antiquities and the Indians who created them.

Hatcher said after a while, "Any fool who'd spend his life in this godforsaken place should have been shut up with a string of spools! Fair gives me the jitters—can't you feel it, Corrigan?"

"It is kind of depressin', sure enough."

"Depressing! Is that all you notice? By Gawd I don't look forward to spending a night here!"

"Guess someone must've filled you with them stories about the chindi."

"Chindi?" he growled suspiciously. "What's that?"

"Spirits of the ancient dead. Must be a

heap of them around. Stands to reason. What the college crowd refers to as original Americans were tramping these localities at least six thousand years before Christ."

Fletcher gasped, goggling, "Jesus! I didn't know he'd ever been around here—"

"Oh, be still," Hatcher said, and brutally kicked his horse into a canter, in a hurry it seemed to catch up with the others. "What's the matter with him?" Fletcher grumbled. "He's been jumpin' around like the seven-year itch."

CHAPTER EIGHT

We camped that night at the canyon's far end where he had two of the crew with the sweat rolling off them go down into the wash and dig a monstrous great pit, deep enough pretty near to bury the whole outfit. We didn't know what Harry was after, but if it was water he sure didn't find any. By the time each horse had drunk a hatful out of our canvas sacks there wasn't enough left, putting them all together, to put out the puny fire Alfredo kindled. "By Gawd, that does it!" Fletcher snarled, glaring at Harry. "What the hell do we do now?"

"Guess you'll have to do without."

"I can open some canned pears," Jones offered with a scathing look at the skimpy fire. "I can open some corned beef but you'll have to eat it cold. I mean, just the way it comes from the tin."

I saw the amusement slide through Fern's glance as she took in the comical look on Hatcher's face. "Go ahead," he growled. "Be better than nothing." His stare swiveled irascibly. "In the morning," he told Clampas, "send a couple of the crew out with rifles and see if they can't scare up some fresh meat."

It was a sour-faced outfit that sought their blankets after wolfing down Jones's provender. Jeff's look, no matter the deserts heat, appeared five shades paler than it had that noon. I could understand his stunned expression for, on top of all the other tribulations, to find ourselves without water and no flowing stream nearer than fifty miles in any direction, everything he had planned was on the brink of disaster. These horses couldn't last long without water. He was faced with the ruin of everything he had hoped for.

"Damn it all," Hatcher muttered, "there's got to be water around here someplace. Along the sides of that wash you could see where floods had almost crept up to more than one of those ruins. Jones, you an' Alfredo get down in that hole and do some more digging!"

Nobody yet had gone out to hunt meat. I hadn't seen one rabbit in the last thirty miles but there were coyotes probably if you could manage to stomach them. I'd noticed signs of ancient irrigation at Una Vida and one or two of the larger pueblos we'd passed, and downslope east of where we'd come into the canyon there might be a spring, though it wasn't a heap likely.

"What about that fork where the canyon branched off in a gulch toward the west?" Jeff asked anxiously. "Perhaps we could find water there . . ."

It was possible of course; anything was possible. I had been intending, if we could shake Harry and his pair of trigger-happy hard cases, to slip Jones and the Larrimores down that arroyo and whatever tinned stuff we could manage to get out with. Branching off of it somewhere along the left side, pretty well hidden last time I'd been through, was another narrow trail with the kind of thing Jeff had been hoping for. Not a large community—perhaps thirty rooms—but in a pretty fair state of preservation and no evidence of vandalism. It even had a small kiva, or ceremonial chamber, I seemed to recollect. And a well you could reach with a long rope and bucket.

I peered around for Flossie. She was not with Fern or anywhere in sight. Jones and Alfredo, armed with shovels and a pick besides, had just reluctantly started for the wash when Fletcher said bitterly, "I'm goin' to git outa here—"

Hatcher swung round. "You'll go when the rest go!"

Seeing the way they were glaring at each other I was mightily tempted to make the big push till I saw Clampas with those pale eyes fixed on me and that black-bored Sharps pointed right at my brisket. Clampas's gaunt cheeks twitched in that high flat face and I turned away, cursing under my breath just as Flossie, coming out of the wash, stopped to shake. Jones's yell came up after her. "Two foot of water in that hole!"

The next hour was spent filling up our water sacks and taking the horses, one by one, down to drink. When the pool cleared a bit I took Gretchen down under Clampas's watchful eye.

"Well," Harry said in his old hearty manner, "what's next on the agenda?"

Jeff still looked unsettled by this change in prospects, like he was finding it hard to pull himself together. "I don't know," he said vaguely, "most everything we've seen either entails more work than I have time for or has been worked over by somebody else. I'd thought," he said, looking north, "to try up there but it doesn't seem very promising . . ."

It certainly didn't: badlands far as the eye could reach, a vast desolation it would take weeks to explore. I couldn't see nothing for it but to take them on back to where that side gulch branched off and try our luck there.

I told him, "That side canyon we passed near that last big pueblo just might have something, or you could try that ruin. I don't think anyone's done a serious study there or done any sort of a scientific dig, though the refuse heaps have been pawed over and vandals—"

"Let's try that side canyon," Jeff said without hope; and Hatcher sent off the crew to pack up the supplies and get the pack string loaded. It was close to ten o'clock before we got out of there.

Every mile—sometimes less—along the canyon's north side there were ruins large or little, and only the most insignificant remains had been bypassed by persons who had been there before us. Since the publication of Lieutenant Simpson's *Journal of Military Reconnaissance from Santa Fe, New Mexico, to the Navajo County*, dude pot hunters and others had prowled through here in ever increasing numbers by what you could reckon from the look of these places.

Some of the towns had practically disappeared save what was left among the rubble of centuries, some battered and broken walls with scarce a foot or two showing above scattered rocks turned black from the heat with hardly a tuft of seared grass showing where once there must have been considerable farming. If the Anasazi had left anything from the time of their occupancy not taken away by those who came later, it would probably be in such near-obliterated remnants as these.

It was well past noon when we reached the branch canyon and started along it with skeptical glances sweeping across the bleak cliffs. "I don't think there's much here," Harry told Jeff with a disgruntled snort.

"We better go back an' try one of them others."

Fern and Jeff exchanged glances near as hopeless as Hatcher's. Gretchen heaved up a sigh. I wanted to suggest Jeff should look a mite farther but thought better of the notion. Hatcher would send someone with him and not like to be me. I said, "Can't be sure, but around that next bend there's another ruined place I seem to remember that might not be too torn up."

Harry shrugged and we pushed on.

There *was* such a ruin and of pretty fair size. Jagged holes had been poked through the nearest wall where looters had busted through in their search for anything they figured worth taking. Harry dismounted, jerking his head at Larrimore. "Rest of you stay here, we're going to have a look."

They'd been gone about ten minutes when we saw them coming back. "Place has been ransacked," Jeff told his sister. "By the shards I picked up it's a long way from old enough to waste any time on. Basketmakers hadn't anything to do with it." He put his look on Harry. "You want to go any farther?"

Harry scowling at me, abruptly made up his mind.

"Might as well," he grumbled, and climbed back into his saddle.

It was a twisty trail, half obliterated, the floor at this point not over a hundred yards wide with the walls closing in and no sign at all of travel. Stunted bushes cropped up here and there, prickly pear and cholla, an occasional ocotillo thrusting up its thorny wands.

Some mile or so beyond that demolished ruin we'd stopped at, the walls opened out again. A lot of rock was strewn about where great sections of the heat-cracked cliff had broken loose to fall among a scraggle of stunted iron-wood. Since leaving the Chaco we'd come four or five miles in what was now little more than a gulch when, greatly astonished, the crew stopped to gape. What we saw was another seep with a ten-foot pool of gleaming water shining under it and tamarisks and salt cedar stretching tall beside it.

Hatcher grunted with a pleased look around. "We'll make camp here an' start back tomorrow."

They got the horses penned after letting them drop their heads for a drink and got busy unloading the pack string. I watered Gretchen and rubbed her down and left her on grounded reins to limp over and help Jeff set up Fern's tent, Flossie watching with her tongue lolling out. Just as Fern ducked through the flap, wiping the sweat off her cheeks, I told her brother as Harry started toward us, "There's a cliff house not two miles from where we're standing."

Hatcher came up with a suspicious stare. "You know this place was here?"

"Figured it was bound to be if it hadn't dried up."

"Why didn't you open your yap about it yesterday?"

"Wasn't too sure we could find it."

"Yeah. I bet." A nastier expression took hold of his mouth. "Don't push your luck, Corrigan. I meant what I told you. If you want to keep healthy, better watch your step." With an angry nod he strode off to join Clampas, who had his back to a rock watching cozily while Alfredo dug out tinned ham from the stores and Jones stirred up dough for the biscuits.

We had a good meal that evening and a medium-sized fire that we could loll around afterward, and the majority of us—except for a guard sent off to stand between us and the way we had come—took a thankful advantage of it. Smoke from hand-rolleds curled and fluttered among the bouquet from Jeff's slim cigar. Flames winked and danced above Jones's bed of ashes. No voice was raised in anger. Talk was sporadic, stretched out and thin until Harry, making a push to get Larrimore started, asked from his place between Fern and me what Jeff thought of the prospects.

"Well, all the ruins we've so far looked at were put up in at least three different time spans. I can't believe even the earliest of these had a great deal to do with the earliest Anasazi, the first influx of Basketmakers. My guess would be they most probably date from Basketmaker Three.

"One has to realize, of course, that all those far-back aborigines didn't come from the same mold—nor fit it. These prehistoric people arrived in this region in successive waves. The first group," Jeff said, warming up to his subject, "are the people I'm most interested in, the original tribe to cross the Bering Strait; primitive, with few skills, who lived in pit houses and built no permanent shelters."

The happy eagerness of Flossie's look as she lay by her mistress and hopefully watched me, occasionally waving the plum of her tail, was the pleasantest view I had seen in some while. Fern's head with its freckled nose and that mop of roan hair was obscured by Hatcher's shoulder between us.

"After them," Jeff went on, "came Basketmaker Two and Three as they're called. Following these at widely separated dates came the Pueblo peoples. The original Basketmakers were nomadic hunters and gatherers who constructed neither pottery nor permanent quarters. Understanding this, it becomes obvious at once that any Basketmaker remains in the Chaco are either deeply buried or the work of Basketmaker Three."

"And so?" said Hatcher.

"So," Jeff replied, "a dig under such considerations and with less than five weeks before I'm expected back in Chicago seems out of the question. An archaeologist of any repute is not one to throw dirt helter-skelter. Much as I hate to, any dig I make here will have to be left to some future date."

"Mean to say," Hatcher growled, "you're throwin' this up and taking off for home?"

"Not precisely. I will do whatever I can to find facts and leave from some point closer than Ajo."

Ears cocked, grinning face on paws and her behind in the air, Flossie was trying to encourage me to play. As Fern had said, the dog evidently liked me. "If that brute," Hatcher said, "tries jumpin' on me it's going to be her last jump!"

Fern took hold of her, pulling the dog back and showing in the scath of her look a bristling indignation as it settled on Harry. "Meantime," Jeff went on, "the most I can hope to pick up in this manner are relics of artifacts from people designated as Basketmaker Three, which really isn't what I came for. And if you're thinking of burial sites," he told Hatcher, "it's been established on pretty good authority these persons also had gone by 1200 A.D., near enough."

There wasn't any of this what Harry wanted to hear and he studied Jeff dourly.

When it occurred to me to take enough stock to find out where the divers personalities of this field trip were placed in relation to the others, I couldn't see Jones and had no idea where Fletcher had got to until I heard him slamming his way through the tamarisks.

Red-faced and panting he came barging up, to gasp out at Harry, "There's a *cliff house* up this trail! Just a whoop and a holler beyond them trees!"

The whole crowd was galvanized. Hatcher jumped up with every other last thing fallen out of his head to go at an accelerating gait in the direction of that water-fed growth as though determined to be the next to see this marvel, the rest of us strung out in his wake and Flossie barking in a seventh heaven of excitement.

Nobody stopped to rope out any mounts and our exodus from camp soon resembled a rout. Fern, as I went past, caught hold of my arm. "Do you suppose that's true?"

"It's true enough. I was hopin' they wouldn't find out about it till your brother had a chance to go over it private."

"You think it's—?"

"Couldn't tell. I been hoping it would fall into the right age bracket—looks older than Moses, and I don't believe any vandals have got to it. Nine chances out of ten that kind of trash would never have pushed through those woods. Been content," I said, "with the discovery of that water and gone back the way they came."

She peered up at me anxiously. "What do you think will happen now?"

"I don't know. Try, if you can, to keep Flossie away from Harry. And away, particularly, from that prize pair of killers."

The goal that had drawn us all like a magnet was still some distance ahead of where

Hatcher and Jeff spearheaded our invasion. Most everyone now had dropped to a kind of shuffling walk though the quiet habitual to this hidden place hung in shuddering tatters in the battering from voice sounds. Jeff's small torch threw monstrous great shadows that continually hopped around us like a band of frightened chindis.

"There!" Fletcher cried. "Right there! Do you *see* it?"

Not even those nearest, pressing forward in the awful grip of ungovernable excitement, managed to conceal this wonder from Fern's riveted gaze. There was a tenseness in her grip, the breath seemed caught in her throat. "It's magnificent!" she whispered. "Just the sort of place Jeff's been praying he could find!"

In the moving light, as the torch was flashed about, the sheer wall built against the cliff's red rock must have reared a full fifty feet above the gulch's passage, unpierced in its lower dimensions. Larrimore, attempting speech through his emotion-blocked throat, was heard to say, "Tomorrow we'll have a good look at it; there's nothing we can reasonably accomplish tonight."

CHAPTER NINE

No one lay abed or lingered beneath cover once the hours of darkness had passed. They were far too excited, too anxious to get inside that relic of ages and learn what sort of treasure had lain hidden here through uncounted years. Not one of the bunch even thought to complain at the refried beans Jones had hashed up to give body to his java.

Harry, in the first bright shaft of the rising sun, appeared as innocently expansive as a con man in possession of his neighbor's billfold. Even Alfredo was grinning as he piled our used breakfast gear into Jones's wreck pan. And Flossie, dancing about, divided her attention between me and her freckled mistress.

All the world was agleam that morning.

Fletcher's muttered claim that he should be given no less than a finder's fee brought a general laugh. Not even Hatcher spoiled it. "What's the procedure?" he inquired of Jeff. "How do we tackle this?"

"First off," Jeff told us, "I think we'd better find some way to get in. And the most important thing to be borne in mind is for the rest of you not to touch anything till I've had a chance to examine the place. Should we move our camp? I ask because if we don't, someone is certainly going to have to keep an eye on it."

"Not me!" Fletcher growled.

"Me neither," spoke up Clampas.

Harry's roving eye pinned Alfredo. "You'll do. Give him Corrigan's rifle. Fletch —you stay here too. I don't want to come back and find this camp all over hell's kitchen."

Fletcher's cheeks locked into anger. Hatcher, ignoring him, bade me go break out a pick and shovel and step lively.

I passed these tools to one of the crew that I knew was too stupid to open his jaw and limped off to throw my saddle on Gretchen, after which I stepped into it. And heard Flossie growl as Harry brushed past her. But Fern had a hold on her so Hatcher went on, increasing his step to catch up with Jeff. "How," he asked, "do we get into this place?"

I kicked a foot from the stirrup and hauled Fern up behind me. "No sense in you walkin' like the rest of these peons." Felt pretty good having her arms around me, and I thought to myself I'd better try this again.

We could see that place a lot plainer with the sun up. Against that red rock it was even more impressive than it had seemed the night before, the whole towering face of it built up from little flat stones. And no openings at all in the lower two thirds of it.

Jeff, standing there with Harry, thoughtfully eyeing it, said, "Looks like we'll have to go in from the top unless we can make out to rig up a ladder—"

"Can't we just knock a hole in it someplace?"

The turn of Jeff's head showed what he thought of that. Fern got off Gretchen's rump and I got out of the saddle, letting go of the reins to stand with the others peering up at that sheer wall.

Trouble was we hadn't any ladder and, as Harry pointed out, no trees tall enough to make one that would be long enough to reach those openings.

Jeff said, "We'll have to send someone up to have a look on top. Bound to be some way of getting inside it. Anyone care to volunteer?"

Nobody clambered over the rest to become the first to get his name remembered.

Hatcher said, "We'll all go then. It's a

cinch there won't nobody get in from down here."

"Time's a-wastin'," I mentioned. "Which way do we go?"

"Straight ahead," Jeff answered. "No way up back there."

I left Gretchen hitched to the ground, glad I'd remembered to throw some oats into her, and took off after the rest of them, expecting to have a pretty stiff hike. Without finding some kind of stairway we'd have to keep on till we found a spot where a section of the cliff had broken off to give us handholds.

It took an hour to come onto one.

And a pretty depressing sight it was, with great chunks of rock tumbled hell west and crooked, just about choking off what was left of this gulch. Catclaw and cholla grown up in tangles all through it. Hatcher led off, warily picking his way with Jeff right behind him, the rest of us strung out and myself helping Fern as seemed only natural at the end of the line.

Getting up took the bulk of another half hour with the sun hammering down and sweat rolling freely to mix with the dust raised by those ahead. "And it looks like," I muttered, "we'll come back the same way!" But one good thing, I thought to myself, at least some of these rannies would have had a bellyful.

We now found ourselves on a kind of plateau with a wide sweep of country stretching off a far piece to a haze of blue hills slithering out of the distance. "Wake up," Fern exclaimed. "Let's not get left here!"

On this high scarp we trudged after the others, presently catching up to hear Hatcher wanting to be told how we'd know when we got there. It was a fair question. The serrated lip of this bluff sure as hell wasn't posted. "I guess," Jeff answered, "well, have to keep looking over."

Harry, snorting, caught hold of one of the crew and with a shove sent him forward. "Get on up ahead an' find that place, Frisco."

Eventually he did. "Right under me now," he called, going abruptly motionless in his crouch above the rim. Hurrying forward I followed his look. Down there beneath us in a scrambling tug of war was a hatless Fletcher on one end of her reins and Gretchen on the other setting back with bared teeth.

"Get away from that mule!"

Fletcher's head spun around, glittery eyes trying to find me. "Up here," I called, and shoved off an egg-sized rock to nudge him. He let out a yell, eyes big as a bull's when he spotted my pistol about to open him up. He let go of those reins in such an explosion of hustle he tripped over his spurs and went down like a tree with all branches crashing.

"D-Don't shoot!" he gasped, a quivering bundle of terror. "Lemme tell—"

Gretchen's raucous complaint sawed the rest of it off just as I felt three-four others crowding back of me, and Hatcher told his henchman, "Never mind the windies!"

Fletcher's weather-roughened features ran together like sloppy dough. "But I come after that mule t' help me find you fellers—"

"A likely tale."

"Like or not," Harry's hard case shouted, "Alfredo's all spraddled out like a bunch of old clothes with a knife buried back of his wishbone. An' I'm tellin' you, by Gawd, there ain't a horse left in camp!"

CHAPTER TEN

You'd have thought we were figures chopped out of wood.

No telling how long we stood clamped in this paralysis staring at the horrid thing that

104

was now spelled out in front of us. Locked in this catastrophe it was Hatcher's snarl that broke our shackles. "Stay right there!" he bellowed, and took off pell-mell over the way we'd just come, the whole crew but Jones going hellity larrup after him.

I found my look on Clampas, who gave me back a cynical grin. "If them broncs are gone they're gone, that's all, and the boys'll hev to chase after them. Me, I stick with the main chance, mister. Right here with the professor."

Jeff, turning away, said, "We've got to find that entrance."

"But Jeff . . ." Fern cried. "If the horses are gone?" She appealed to me with her eyes seeming black against the pallor of that freckled skin.

"Like Clampas I'm stringin' along with Jeff." I dropped a hand on her shoulder. "Buck up. We're like to be here a right smart while before those horses become important."

She eyed me uncertainly. "That poor man . . ."

"Very sad." Clampas nodded without visible grief. "These things happen. A business of this sort is hazardous at best."

She twisted around to have a sharp look

at him. He stood there smiling in the best Hatcher fashion but making no attempt to dress it up in fine linen. "One learns to adjust."

Quite true, I thought, but no need to be so blunt about it. Fern moved closer to me. "But how could it happen? Who do you suppose killed him?"

"You want it tied up in pink ribbons?" Clampas shifted his weight. His glance touched mine. "I wouldn't put it past Fletch . . ."

With a look of abhorrence she turned her back on him. But, it came over me, there'd been no one else down there. Still, in a larger view, this *could* have been something handsome Harry dreamed up, using Fletch for the cat's-paw. . . .

Jeff, with no heed for us, was down on one knee picking at the cliff's edge with his silver-handled jackknife. Grunting now he stood up, slipping the knife back into his pocket. "I believe this end has been built up with masonry. Take a look at it, Brice. Built up and smoothed and made to look solid rock with some kind of reddish mud plaster."

Now that I looked closer, I could see what he meant. The top of the bluff where we stood, the end nearest Chaco Canyon that is, for eight or ten feet felt different to the touch. "Let me have that shovel," Jeff said, and proceeded gingerly to scratch at the surface.

He'd guessed right. It was some sort of mud mortar artfully plastered over a cunningly contrived sheet of masonry. Long ago it seemed likely a fairly large chunk had fallen out of the cliff at this point. "This has to be where the entrance was—there's no other place for it," Jeff panted, busily scaling off that whole stretch of plaster to uncover the work of men long gone. "When they quit this building they did their best to conceal the way in. Look there," he pointed. "It's a kind of blind window they've laid up across what used to be the doorway. When everything was ready they simply filled this in."

It seemed plain enough now he'd pointed it out.

"You'll notice," he said, "when they sealed this up they set the rocks in vertically instead of crossways like the rest of this stretch; it proved handier I suppose."

"How you reckon to get in there?" I asked.

"We'll have to be careful. I certainly don't want to break this up. What we need right here is something we can use to poke out the mud between those upright stones. A case knife or bowie—"

"I've got a bowie," Jones said, stepping forward. "Let's have a look at that."

Jeff made room and Jones, kneeling, began to pick at the binder. It appeared to have hardened considerably through uncounted ages, though in some spots it had deteriorated noticeably. After about twenty minutes of steady digging, the rock he was working on let go and fell with an echoing rumble and clatter into whatever lay directly beneath.

Jeff motioned Jones aside to put his face to the hole. "Blacker than pitch," he said. "I can't see a thing. Try the next stone," he muttered, getting out of the way. "You'll have to admit," he remarked as Jones resumed his labors, "those old boys were indefatigable workers. They must have quarried, transported and tediously shaped several million stones in the building of this place. A prodigious task with the primitive tools available to them; at least as difficult, I would imagine, as the construction of the Egyptian pyramids."

At the end of half an hour Jones had three more stones out, the last pair caught and gruntingly laid to one side. "Not quite so dark down there now."

Jeff, taking his place, peered into the hole for a nerve-rasping spell. Fern asked, "Can you see anything?"

"Not much," Jeff muttered, getting up to stretch his back. "Near as I could tell, there's a five-or six-foot drop. Probably know more about it once we get the rest of these stones lifted out."

"Let me take a whack at it," I said, and Jones passed me the knife.

It soon became evident that, because of the weight and the awkwardness of how we had to go about it, you couldn't remove but one stone at a time without risk of damaging whatever was below. Between us during my stint with the knife Jones and I managed to get out three more of the stones used to seal up the entrance. This left only four more in place when we moved back to give Jeff another look.

"Well," he told us as he got to his feet, "what we're faced with is a narrow room some four feet high, every wall of which is plastered and without any sign of an opening except for the one we've just made."

"Oh dear," Fern exclaimed. "You mean it doesn't go anywhere?"

"There'll be a door, I'm sure, or another blind window, but we're going to have to hunt for it." He considered it, frowning. "We're not going to get into that place today." He took a squint at the sun. "We'd better get back to the camp while there's still light."

We built up the fire while Jones dug a hole in the dwindling pile of our supplies and Flossie quartered the site with her nose to the ground, dashing first one way and then off at a tangent. I led the hee-hawing Gretchen to the pool for a drink, then fetched her back and hung a nosebag on her. Hatcher and his horse hunters weren't anywhere in sight, nor was the corpse of Alfredo, which I reckoned they must have buried.

Jones opened several tins of ham, got out his Dutch oven and started working up dough for his biscuits. Fern peeled potatoes and sliced them into a bowl while Jeff sat figuring on a page of his blue-backed notebook. The sun was gone and it was getting dark fast when a strengthening sound of travel pulled all eyes in the direction of the trail.

Looking pretty well beat, Hatcher and his

helpers came up to the fire. No one ventured to prod them with questions for all could see there were no horses with them. Hatcher said finally, "No we didn't find them. I reckon them ponies must've run halfway to the canyon."

You couldn't hardly call Jones's fine supper a hilarious occasion. Hatcher perked up a mite when told we'd uncovered the entrance to our objective. No one sat around the fire once the meal was finished. Off to one side Clampas beckoned Harry for a low-voiced conversation with several frowning looks in the direction of Fletcher, and a short time later—Harry having put two of the crew on guard with Clampas—the rest crawled into their blankets.

Despite the daytime heat, which must have been topping out at close to a hundred, the nights were cool and, toward morning, often rightdown chilly. Though strongly tempted to hitch Gretchen, in the end I did not do so but fetched her under the tamarisks and there made my bed. Not that I expected to get a lot of sleep.

A jumble of thoughts juned around in my noggin, fleeting visions of Fletch in his various attitudes interwoven with sundry pictures of Harry. Having Gretchen, thoughts of the horses did not unduly worry me. For once Jeff made up his mind to depart, we could strike out for Farmington on the Denver & Rio Grande, not over fifty miles away. About two days by shanks' mare. I could put Fern on Gretchen.

I probably dozed, off and on, but in more wakeful moments I kept coming back to the unexplainable raid on our horses. Who but Fletcher could have set that in motion? The man was mercurial enough for just about anything, yet the suspicion kept nagging me that Hatcher might have been back of it, that a couple of those nags might not have left with the rest. Once Harry got his hands on any loot of real importance he would be long gone in one hell of a hurry.

If any off-color business got afoot during the night I certainly wasn't aware of it.

I did not wake at the crack of dawn, but came alive shortly after to the aroma of coffee and the sight of Turtle Jones hunched over his fire-blackened skillet. Jeff and Clampas were already stirring and it looked like being another hot day.

Gretchen was happily browsing on such tufts of grass as she could find about the pool and, looking around with lifted head, gave me a cheerful gate-hinge greeting which could hardly have failed to rouse the whole camp. "Well," Hatcher growsed, untangling himself from his bedroll, "does that godforsaken critter have to wake us every day!"

Flossie slipped out of Fern's tent and with great aplomb came to a squat behind the closest bush. She then cantered round with her nose to the ground taking inventory of any new smells the night had left behind, vigorously flailing her tail when she caught sight of me, further expressing her delight by hustling over to jump about with much enthusiasm, never quite touching me. "Good girl!" I said, and she ran off to find Fern.

Jones yelled, "Come'n get it!"

We wasted no time in putting it away. Returning from dropping our tools into the washtub, Jeff said to Hatcher, "Off to more horse hunting, are you?"

"Not me," Harry declared. "That bunch —if they ain't been stole and spirited out of the country—will probably wind up makin' Navajo stew!" His glance checked Jeff's face. "I been talkin' to Clampas—think you'll get into that place today?"

"The date of our entry," Larrimore told him, "could be anybody's guess. People who put up that apartment house went to some pains to close it up when they left. All of yesterday's work didn't get us any farther than a completely sealed room."

"Don't pay to be too particular. Bust a hole through the wall and you're on your way."

Jeff shook his head. "I wish it were that simple. I think I'll borrow Jones again if you've no objection."

"Good worker, is he?"

"Opening up that house in an acceptable manner," Jeff said, "requires skill and know-how, not just muscle. Far as I can tell, no looters or pot hunters have got inside yet. Which makes it imperative," he went earnestly on, "that I allow nobody in there but authorized personnel." He stopped to give Hatcher a very straight look.

Harry gave it back to him. "Suits me," he said, and grinned. "I authorize Clampas to be your chief helper."

Young Larrimore showed him a wintry smile. He knew as well as Harry there was no getting around it, that whatever Hatcher wanted there was nothing to stand in his way.

He took a deep breath. "Do I get Jones too?"

"Sure. Take anyone you want. I think we understand each other," Harry said smugly.

Fern, coming up, asked, "Couldn't someone manage to construct a ladder? With all those trees . . ."

"Yes, ma'am." Harry trotted out his charm to affably assure her, "I'll see what I can do."

As before, I took Fern up behind me on Gretchen; Clampas, Jeff and Jones took to hoofing it. And once more, as before, I left Gretchen standing below the great wall and limped on with the others to the place of fallen rock. It must have been about nine by the time we stood before the hole we'd made in the entryway yesterday. There were still the four stones we had yet to prize out of it. Jones picked up his bowie and went methodically to work.

"What is Harry," Jeff said to Clampas, "going to do about those horses?"

"What *can* he do?" Clampas shrugged with spread hands. "When you're ready to go we'll just have to walk. We can probably make Farmington in a couple of days. You can catch a train there." He eyed Jeff curiously. "What I can't savvy is why you picked Ajo to take off on this jaunt."

Larrimore said grimly, "I left the arrangements up to Harry."

No more breath was wasted on talk until Jones and me had got those four stones out and carefully laid them outside the hole. At that point Jeff said, "You go first, Corrigan."

Not sure how much of a drop there might be in that uncertain light, I took my time and went in belly down with considerable care, remembering the stones we'd dropped in there yesterday. "How's it look?" Jeff called with his head through the hole.

"Not much room to work in down here. Anybody think to fetch that bar?"

"We've got it right here." He passed it down and I handed up the loose rocks that cluttered the floor. Jeff said, "I'm coming down," and stood a few moments after he had joined me, taking a long look around. "Not much headroom," he grunted.

"No. You'll have to watch out for your head. They did a good job—not a crack in these walls. Where do we start?"

He stood awhile, cogitating, mulling it over. "Let's see . . . that left-hand wall will probably open into space. Chances are we'd best tackle this one. And low down, Brice—about two feet up from the floor and close to this end where it connects with the cliff."

I picked up the bar, driving the chisel end into the plaster. Nothing came of the impact other than the merest splatter of dust and the negligible mark the bar had left on the wall. I looked at Jeff. "Go ahead," he said. "Try it again. A little more to the right."

Same story. "Feels like solid rock."

Jeff nodded. "Probably is. Try a bit higher."

I did, but no improvement. I banged the bar into it again, lower this time. It went in about two inches and when I jerked it out about twelve inches of plaster flaked off. No seams showed behind it. "They've set a single rock upright," Jeff said, "to seal off the passage. See if you can scale off some more of that plaster."

Starting at floor level and working upward, I cleared a space some three feet by five and when the dust finally settled we had ourselves a look. What they had done was plain enough now. As Jeff had surmised, they had set in an upright slab of rock measuring two feet by three. "Be just about big enough," I said, "to let us squeeze through. Once we've got that slab pried loose."

"How about givin' me a turn with that bar?"

"You bet!" I said and, with the sweat dripping off my chin, was glad to climb out. "Whew!" I puffed, flipping Jones a wink. "You can have my next turn. Talk about Turkish baths—that's got them all beat!"

"Not much room." Jones grinned.

"Toss down that knife," Clampas grunted. "I've got to loosen this mortar."

Pretty soon Jeff said, "Try it now." We could see Clampas laying into it with that forty-pound bar, bent over like a gnome to keep his head off the ceiling. He'd got out of his shirt and even in that half light you could see the gleaming roll of huge muscles and the way they jumped every time that bar slogged home. A steel-driving man if ever I saw one.

"Stand back," he grunted some five minutes later. "I think it's moved—couple more whacks and it's goin' to come out of there." He spat on his hands and took a new grip.

"A genuine pleasure," Jones breathed in my ear, "to be up here watchin' that feller at work."

"You bet," I said, "and it's something you ain't like to see every day. I'd admire to give Fletch a dose of the same!"

"*Look out!*" Clampas hollered. There was a grating wrench and a resounding crash and through the dust I could just make out that great whopping slab laying flat on the floor.

"Bravo!" Jones cried, and we both clapped hands.

Clampas grinned up at us. Jeff pulled his head back out of the new hole. "Can't see a thing. Pass down that torch."

Jones put it in Clampas's lifted hand and he and Jeff moved over to the opening, pointing the light on whatever lay beyond. They took a good long look, so long Jones growled impatient, "Hell's fire! Cat got your tongues?"

Jeff shook his head. "Another empty room. Bigger than this but otherwise just like it."

I guessed he was pretty disgusted after all that work and so little to show for it. "Go ahead—take a look," Jeff said. Clampas wiggled his length through the hole he'd just opened, disappearing from sight. Jones lit a smoke. Jeff stepped over to the hole. "Just the same?" he called.

Clampas's voice when it reached us had a faraway sound. "Just the same, except size. Plaster on every wall. Not a crack showing. What the hell time is it?"

I consulted my shadow. "Round about three." Jones looked at his watch. "Three-twenty." I said, "Where's Fern?"

"She went back a couple hours ago. Guess she got hungry—which reminds me," Jones said. "I prob'ly better be gettin' back too."

"Guess we all had," Jeff said as Clampas rejoined him. "Too late to get through another wall today. Anyway this torch needs fresh batteries."

Some things, I thought, can't hardly be mistaken.

We were bound for camp, picking our way through the catclaw and cholla garnishing that fall of tumbled rock, grim of eye and thin of lip, nobody opting for conversation, each of us turning things over in private. Peering at Jeff as we moved along, one could not help noticing the harried expression that in the past several days looked to be coming habitual. I suspected this sample of life in the real world had descended on him as a pretty rugged jolt.

He must have found Harry a rude disappointment, to have discovered in the man an unscrupulous schemer where he'd looked for a knowledgeable enthusiastic friend. To realize he'd hired a purveyor of illusions must have been a sad shock. Even more than the affront to his self-esteem had been the growing conviction his whole trip had been wasted unless something of value could be dug out of this cliff house.

Clampas, I reckoned, would have been a pleasant surprise. The way the man had pitched in, the prodigious work he had done could have given Jeff assumptions which had no basis in fact. Absorbed in his own concerns, determined on the renown which must so far have eluded him, Larrimore was in no condition to see Clampas as I saw him—hard, twisted, coldly calculating, a man without sentiment who would kill even quicker than that lout of a Fletcher if it suited his purpose.

I was glad I didn't stand in Hatcher's boots.

We were back at camp, pushing through the tamarisks about the pool when Jeff in the lead stopped with such suddenness Jones banged into him. No need to search for the cause of their astonishment. It was there in plain sight.

The horses were back.

CHAPTER ELEVEN

Back, too, was the Navajo, Hosteen Joe, the man who had left our hospitality in fury, that brash young buck who had wanted Clampas's rifle.

Hobnobbing with Harry, plump with smiles and self-importance, proudly fastened to my confiscated Remington, Joe had the strut of a visiting chief. Harry, too, looked to be in fine fettle as he beckoned us forward in his heartiest manner.

"Look who's here and see what he's fetched us—every last pony that departed this camp!"

No mention, I noticed, of poor old Alfredo.

"What happened?" Clampas asked. "Couldn't he find a buyer?"

"That's no way to make a man welcome," Harry chided. "Took him three days to get these broncs rounded up."

"Yeah," I said. "What's he doing with my rifle?"

"Not to worry. We gave him that as a very small token of our appreciation." Turning to Jones he said, "See if you can't dish up something extra special tonight. You know —in honor of the occasion, eh?"

Jones without answering went off toward the fire some jubilant soul had thoughtfully built up for him and began rattling round among his pots and pans.

Fern with Flossie scampering alongside came over to ask her brother what he'd found. "Well," she remarked after his unenthusiastic answer, "that's encouraging, don't you think? They'd hardly have gone to so much trouble if they'd left nothing behind other persons might value."

"Perhaps you're right," Jeff nodded dourly, and tried then to show a more cheerful countenance. "It's not the work of the original Basketmakers, but it may well prove to have been constructed by some of the descendants not too far removed. It doesn't have the appearance of Pueblo work."

I sensed an anxious look of foreboding in her glance as Clampas came up to consider her blandly. "Not worrying about the chindis, are you? After all these years there shouldn't be much left of them."

Jones outdid himself with supper that night. Baked potatoes and ham, johnnycake and java hot from the coffee-pot with juicy canned Bartlett pears to wind up with. Harry pronounced it a feast fit for kings.

Hosteen Joe was feeling his oats. "By myself I catch these horses. Not many peoples could do such thing—you know that? Me, I'm one smart Indian, no?"

"You're a wonder." Clampas smiled.

"That hat still fit all right?" Jones asked.

I went off to palaver with Gretchen. Before I got out of earshot Hatcher told Larrimore, "Tomorrow I'm going up there with you. We'll leave Clampas in camp to keep an eye on our belongin's." When Jeff made no comment Harry divulged as though dispensing a favor, "We'll take Fletch along to take care of the rough work."

Gretchen cocked an ear when I stopped beside her and twisted her head to nuzzle my pocket, pulling back her lip while ogling me with great expectation. "Such a moocher," I said as she lipped the sugar lump off my palm.

But I was bothered in my mind, uneasy as Fern, thinking about that Indian fetching back our horses. It seemed a most unlikely action. Why had he done it? What was he up to? I reckoned we'd find out before we got done with this. But, I remembered as I got into my blankets, it was the Sharps Joe had wanted. . . .

Had Joe killed Alfredo? Then stampeded the horses?

It didn't appear to make any great amount of sense to do these things and then fetch them back again. Could he have brought them back to make Hatcher feel beholden? Hatcher was pleased enough to give him my rifle. But it hadn't been mine Joe had taken such a shine to. . . .

Much as I distrusted Clampas, I could think of no way he could have mixed into this. He'd been with us up there on the cliff-top when those broncs had left camp and Alfredo at that point had certainly been alive. Now the horses were back and that Navajo with them. And if Harry had sense enough to pound sand down a rat hole, he'd surely be bright enough to watch that Indian.

I was back in my thinking to that notion Clampas had pushed out for our scrutiny, that Fletcher was the one we should have had our sights on. Had Fletch driven off our caballos on orders from Harry? Then again, if Hatcher'd had no part in it what could Fletch have hoped to gain?

It must have been about there that sleep overtook me.

Next morning, after getting outside Jones's refried beans, I took Gretchen along to the pool for a drink. Coming back with a bucketful to leave outside Fern's tent, I stopped to exchange a few words with Jeff and asked if Fern was going with us this morning. Jeff said, "I suppose so," and frowned. "Must get pretty tedious for her up there but she's refused to stay in camp if that hard-eyed gunslinger is going to be staying here—says he makes her skin crawl. You don't think he'd—?"

"Clampas," I said, "has got his sights set on loot. Same as Harry. It's occurred to me, Jeff, we should have been posting a guard up there."

He peered at me wide-eyed and vigorously nodded. "You're absolutely right. We'll do it hereafter." He stood there thinking about it, then said with a grimace, "Here comes Harry. Guess we better get up there."

"You go ahead. We'll come along as soon as Fern's ready."

It didn't take long to put the saddle on Gretchen. I knew she was not real keen on carrying double but reckoned another sugar lump would improve her outlook. When

Fern came out of the tent to join us I could see she was troubled. She said, "I've this frightful feeling we're heading into something that had better been left alone. Do you suppose, Brice, it was never intended that we should get into that sealed-up place?"

"It's just the strangeness—"

"I feel so alone," she said, looking out over the sunlit surroundings. "This landscape's so big, so bare, it depresses me."

There didn't seem to be very much I could say to that. Flossie then came gamboling up and we got aboard Gretchen and took off for the cliff house, catching up with the others just short of the rockfall.

"Didn't you mean to leave Gretchen back—"

"I'm going to leave her up here where there's something she can browse on. You go ahead. I'm goin' to take the saddle off. Give her a chance to roll if she wants to."

She went off with Flossie eagerly beside her. Jeff, Harry, Jones and Fletcher were halfway to the rim when Fern with a scream abruptly froze in her tracks. I made a pass at my hip and shot the head off the rattlesnake coiling on the sun-bright rock just ahead of her. "You're not going to faint, are you?" I kicked the wriggling mass off the rock.

"No . . ." She looked kind of peaked. "No—of course not!"

"I'll go ahead," I said. "You step where I've stepped."

Jeff, alarmed by the shot, had stopped and was looking back at us. "Snake?" Harry asked, and I nodded. "He didn't get a chance to strike," I assured Jeff. "Gave her a turn—she'll be all right."

At the site of our labors Jones and Fletch were looking things over, Fletch wanting to know how far we had got. "Then you haven't found anything yet," he sneered. "If," he said, "there's anything to *be* found."

Jeff ignored this. "Jones, I expect you remember how we tackled that first room? I want you and Fletcher to get into that second one and get enough of that plaster off to find us a door."

Jones picked up the shovel and followed Fletcher into the hole, then reached up a hand. "Might's well take that bar along, too. We're sure goin' to need it."

It was not long before we heard the shovel flaking off plaster and Hatcher demanding to know if we aimed to spend the day improving our tan. Jeff gave the fellow a very cool look and suggested if Hatcher wasn't entirely happy to be an onlooker on this important occasion no one would insist that he remain standing about.

A startled, half-furious expression skidded across Harry's widely opened stare. A flush, rapidly darkening, crept above his collar as he backed off a couple steps, mouth opening and shutting but with nothing coming out.

Larrimore turned away. "How's the dust down there?" he called into the excavation.

"Not too bad," Jones called back. "There's room enough here if you want to come down. We've got the baked mud off two of the walls." His voice grew less intelligible. Then, much louder, he informed, "Fletch is clearing the wall to the right of our opening—*I believe we're on to something!*"

Flossie barked and disappeared into the clifftop opening. "I'm going down," Jeff said, and followed the dog. "Oh—I do hope they've found something," Fern declared excitedly.

Harry, bending, tried to discover what was going on below. I said, "You can't see where they're at from up here; the place we pulled that slab from is at right angles to the hole you've got your head in."

Fern's hand gripped my arm. Jeff called

up, "They've cleared the third wall and there's a real five-by-two-foot door just waiting for us to get at it. Come down if you want to have a look."

Hatcher wasn't one to step aside for women and children. Thrusting a leg through the hole he lost no time in dropping onto the next level, the four-foot-high room we'd got into a couple days ago. Not wanting her to skin a leg or otherwise collect a hurt I reached up and brought Fern safely down, observing the excited look on her face. "Watch out for your head in this cubbyhole," I muttered, noticing with pleasure the way her nose wrinkled up beneath that mop of roan hair.

Jeff was in the next room with Jones and big Fletch with Harry just beyond the hole we'd made yesterday. "Move over," I told him. "We'd like to see, too."

When we'd all got in there Jeff gestured toward the sealed wooden door they had just uncovered. I was surprised to notice that while it showed considerable age, as might have been expected, it was still a sturdy obstacle. Jeff said, "You're probably about as curious as I am, and I'll admit the desire to tear down this door and get beyond it is almost irresistible. But no reputable archaeologist can afford to give in to that kind of action. There's a meticulous discipline to the way we do things."

He gave Jones a nod and our cowpuncher cook unlimbered his bowie knife and with tedious care began chipping away at the ages-old mortar that held the door shut. "When this was set into the wall," Jeff informed us, "hinges as we know them had not been invented, nor had iron been discovered. What we have here is a solid sheet of wood chopped from a tree with some sort of stone implement, set into the opening and held in place by wedging it with a mud-base mortar filled with tiny pebbles. Once that's been removed the door can be lifted out."

You could see the impatience on those watching faces and I could feel it in myself. It put a strain on our tempers, honed our expectations. By the time the door moved and was brought away in Jones's hands every one of us, I guess, was about ready to pop. First through the opening was Flossie, then Harry Hatcher. We were all crowded around the opening, staring with an intensity that must have been laughable to anyone not caught up in our emotions. The frozen expressions on those roundabout faces were as plain as they were comical. There was nothing to be seen in the uncertain light and that tomblike quiet but another empty room with an open doorway off the left wall.

"Jesus!" Hatcher said. "I might's well have stayed in camp!"

Jeff, stepping forward without remark, crossed the room to the open doorway, through which Flossie had just disappeared. And there he stopped.

To the rest of us, watching in that unearthly quiet broken only by the patter of the dog's clawed feet, there was an arrested quality in Jeff's stance that put, I think, a quivering chill into all of us.

Frustration thinned Jeff's voice when he said, "Nothing in there but a pile of loose sand and off in one corner a hole in the floor."

CHAPTER TWELVE

Hatcher crossed the room with Fletch at his heels, roughly shouldering Jeff out of the way. The dog barked somewhere as they passed out of sight. "Here, Flossie!" Jeff called as the rest of us joined him, but the dog didn't come. We could see Fletcher and Harry crouched over the hole, light from below shining bright on their faces, on dropped jaws and bulged eyes. "Oh—what is it?" Fern cried. "What are you staring at?"

In a stunned tone of voice Harry said, "Damned if I know . . . a lot of stuff down there, all piled up in a corner. Bunch of different-size pots . . ."

Jeff looked disgusted. "The Basketmakers weren't potters." Fern pushed past him. "Do you see Flossie?"

Harry said, "Yeah, she's down there."

"Is she all right?"

"Looks all right to me."

"Let me have a look at those pots," Jeff grunted as we all ganged up behind Fletch and Harry. "What color are they?"

"Black on white," Fletch mumbled.

I said, "Looks to me like they're all Anasazi. They weren't made yesterday, that's for sure. I see a couple of storage jars and what seems like a wedding pot. There's a low flat bowl—maybe these people were Mogollons or some of the late Cochise people. That bowl looks to be about half full of corn."

Said Jeff, like he was turning it over, "Might possibly be Cochise. They made pottery after contact with some of the Mexican Indians."

"How," asked Fern, "are we going to get Flossie out of there?"

"That's about a five-foot drop," Jones said. "We can easy make a ladder—"

"We'll probably have to make several ladders," Jeff said, looking around, "if we don't come across some, which we probably will. We'll have to have short ladders to find out what we've got here. Must be at least five floors to this place."

Fern said to me, "Can't you get Flossie and hand her up?"

"You bet," I said, but after I dropped down there Flossie proved elusive. She'd come up to me and sniff in what seemed a friendly fashion, but each time I tried to get a hand on her she'd duck away.

"You go," Fern said to Jeff. "She'll let you pick her up."

"We'll get her tomorrow," said her brother. "Spending the night here isn't going to hurt her. Tomorrow we'll have a ladder."

I said, "What time you got, Jones?"

"Pretty close to two, about three minutes till."

Harry, catching on, said, "Fletch, you hike back to camp and fetch us a ladder."

There was very little enthusiasm in the

scowl Fletcher showed but muttering under his breath he went back through the hole we had taken the door from. Yet, oddly enough, his departure did not erase the anxious look from Fern's face.

This room I was in was lighter than the upper ones by reason of the window hole that was in the outside wall. There was an elongated shaft of sunlight on the floor and Flossie with her tongue lolling out was sitting in this watching me. "Come on, Flossie," I said, bending toward her. I held out a sugar lump. Her tail thumped the floor but she showed no intention of coming any nearer.

Jones said, "Reckon I better be gettin' back too. I ought to go over that tinned stuff. All this heat . . . you never know. Maybe I can help put together that ladder."

Jeff gave him rather detailed instructions and some ten minutes later he set out. "Keep a lookout for snakes," Jeff called after him.

Fern, still with that anxious look in her eyes, appeared to be keeping a close watch on Flossie, who had gone back to sniffing around that bunch of old pots. Larrimore heaved a despondent sigh. I said, "This place looks to be in pretty good condition. No sign of them—I mean the folks that built it—having been attacked or driven out. If they'd been hit by a plague—"

"It doesn't seem to have been that," Jeff said, shaking his head. "If it's corn in that bowl it couldn't have been lack of water. Perhaps they had a lemming complex, or just an itch to move. Let me look at that bowl, Brice."

I limped over to where Flossie was still nosing the collection, picked up the bowl and passed it up to him. "It's corn. Hard enough to be petrified."

But it wasn't the corn that concerned Jeff. It was the container he was studying.

"Does the design tell you anything?"

"Not really. It was obviously made a long time ago. It's a lightning design repeated with variations through hundreds of years; you'll still see its use in some of the pueblos. It's Anasazi ware, you were right about that. We might get a relative date from that corn."

"How many rooms do you reckon we've got here?"

"Possibly thirty. I wouldn't guess more than that. Probably less."

Flossie came over, stretched out a yawn and sat down beside me, thumping her tail as we exchanged looks. Then she was up again, moving off a few feet to stand intently staring at the door hole opening out of the west wall. Just above a whisper Fern said, "She's listening to something. You don't suppose there's anyone. . . ?"

"Not unless," Jeff said, "there's another way of getting in that we haven't found."

While he was talking I started toward that across-the-room doorway. This was all the encouragement Flossie needed. At a bound she was off and through the opening, the sound of her flying feet rapidly fading. I passed through after her and through three more, pulling up, gun in hand, before a fourth doorway hung with strung beads.

In the breathless quiet I caught the sound of her again, growing plainer. I heard her shake. And then there she was coming out of the beaded doorway, giving a wag of her tail as she sighted me. "Good girl!" I said as she stood looking up at me. "Guess you must've been chasing a chindi."

Jeff, when we got back, was down in the room below Fern, looking over that pile of pots with an expression I felt was unduly thoughtful. "Each of those two largest storage jars," he said, pointing, "are filled with white and black beads. And that pitcher is filled with blue ones."

I picked up the pitcher and poured out a

handful. "Fossil turquoise, and enough of it here to gladden Harry's heart. Prime grade, I'd say—and, by the way, where *is* Harry?"

"He went up top to watch for the ladder."

I poured the handful of turquoise back where it came from. "What do you want to do? Let Harry and friends get a look at this and we're going to have trouble."

"Yes." Jeff grimaced. "Throw a handful of those white beads on top of them and put that pitcher at the back of the pile. We'll have to figure some way to keep them out of sight."

Hoisting myself up till I got a knee hooked over the hole's edge, I climbed out onto Fern's level. "Poor Flossie," Fern said, looking sorrowfully down at her. "Poor, poor Flossie."

"Yes," Jeff said. "Well, shall we go outside? If we had Clampas here he would say his heart bleeds for her."

"You staying down there?" I said.

"I want to poke around a bit. And if you've no objections I'd like you to count on staying here tonight. If we can keep them from it I'd like to keep the vandals in our party from taking over."

I looked up at the sound of running steps approaching. I could feel the whole length of me tightening up. Was this what Fern felt? This queer foreboding? It was like receiving a telegram just as you're about to tuck into your supper. It was Harry, of course, and one glance at his face told us this was no joke.

The words tumbled out of him. "I sent Jones on to camp. Fletch is down in that rockfall with an arrow in his throat!"

CHAPTER THIRTEEN

I left Fern with Hatcher and went hurrying along the clifftop, grimly wondering if this was a second installment of what had been started with Alfredo's death and the stampede of our horses. I wasn't far into those rocks when I found him, face down in the hollow between two large boulders.

You generally know when you're looking at death. There's something about it that makes itself manifest. I knew at first glance Fletcher'd cashed in his chips. I climbed down there and turned him over, wondering what had given Harry the notion an arrow had done for him. Then I saw it and guessed you could call it an arrow if that suited you.

It was there in his throat just below the

Adam's apple, a slender shaft no more than eight inches long, almost certainly propelled from some kind of blowgun. There wasn't much blood.

I took Fletcher's pistol, thrust it into my waistband. No sign of his rifle. If an Indian had done this there wouldn't be. But what kind of Indian around here used a blowgun? Clampas would have said, "Must've been one of them chindis."

This wasn't going to help Jeff's hunt for glory. Our three-man crew was like to cut for the tules when they glommed on to this. If they'd take that smartass Navajo with them . . . A small palaver with Hosteen Joe, it occurred to me, would be at least a possible move in the right direction. Given his make-up . . . We knew nothing at all about the bugger . . . Well, I knew in my own mind Joe was a troublemaker, a rebel and misfit who felt he had been shortchanged in life's lottery. Joe in a number of ways looked cut from the same cloth as Harry—out for any-thing he could get. And not particular how he got it.

If I'd been bossing this deal I'd have run him out—him, Harry and Clampas—and the sooner the better.

I left Fletch where he was and limped

down to see about Gretchen. She didn't like showing it but I could tell she was glad to see me. I gave her a sugar lump and threw on my saddle and, after rummaging my notions, climbed aboard and headed for camp. And got there just as Jones, toting a short ladder, came bucking his way through the tamarisks. "I'll take it," I told him. "Guess the camp's fair buzzin' with the news of Fletch's passing."

"Ain't too much bein' said but plenty wild looks are bein' chucked about." Jones grinned. "Clampas allows the chindis must've got him."

"I thought he'd get around to that. Well, keep your eyes skinned. I'll be stayin' up top tonight, me an' the mule here."

"What about grub?"

"Won't be the first time I've missed the wagon." I hooked an arm through the ladder and gave Gretchen the go sign.

When we reached the rockfall I got down with the ladder and looped the reins around the horn. "You're a smart enough critter to get up there if you've a mind to," I told her. "Just watch your step and follow my lead."

She hee-hawed a couple of times, then took after me. Figuring he'd earned it we bypassed the place where Fletch was resting.

141

I guess she found it rough going but five minutes after I came out on top Gretchen joined me, nuzzling my pocket like she understood her due. Wrapping her lip around a sugar lump beat everything.

She kind of rolled her eyes when she came up to the entrance we had made in that cliff house. You didn't have to spell things out for her; she could read body language and was quick to catch on. I called out to alert the Larrimores, and then told Gretchen, "Browse up here anyplace you've a mind to," and stripped off my gear and cached it just inside that four-foot room that once had served as an entryway.

I found Fern and Jeff in the room above Flossie and set up the ladder. "Be a little careful with this thing, it's not an A-1 job. When the red brothers set out to put a ladder together they lash each joint with a strip of wet hide. Once that dries, you got a real foundation. Well, there you are."

"Jeff," Fern said, "go fetch up Flossie." Then, to me she said, wrinkling up her freckled nose, "I can't stand this place. There's something about it that makes me squirm."

Her brother fetched Flossie up and set

the dog down. She went straight to Fern, wriggling all over, tail threshing ecstatically.

"I'm going to leave this torch with you," Jeff said, putting it into my hand. "Who do you suppose killed that fellow? And with a blowgun! I never heard of our kind of Indians—"

"You never heard of Hosteen Joe till you came out here and met him. I'm not sayin' he did it. Jones tells me Clampas has been laying it on the chindis. First thing you know—Well, never mind that."

"You think he believes it?"

"No. Local tradition tends to back him up, though. You'll find these abos set a great deal of store on that sort of thing. Good excuse for pretty near anything."

Jeff shook his head. "Next year," he said with a determined glance. "I'll come back and find out where these people went. And I'll be bringing my own crew with me!"

"They'll be your kind of people and that makes sense. Have a better grasp of what you're tryin' to accomplish."

He rummaged my face with a sharpened glance. "You've had an education—"

"Sure. School of Hard Knocks. My old man had his own set of notions, didn't subscribe to such dodderin' thoughts as all work and no play makes Jack a dull boy. I got the hell away from him quick as I was able."

"Still," said Jeff, running a thoughtful tongue across his mouth, "some of his lore must have rubbed off on you. That turquoise we found . . ."

"Fossil stuff. Formed as a mineral replacement in reeds, pithy sticks and the like. It's tubular—fine stuff for makin' necklaces."

"Valuable?"

"Rare," I said, "and like most rare things at the changing of hands the price goes up and it's strictly hard cash. How are you figurin' to go over this place? An overall look to see where you're at, or room by room?"

"In the time available I think I'd better see the whole layout first."

"All right then; I'll see you in the morning and we'll get right at it."

Fern's look lingered briefly and then they were gone.

I went out to see how Gretchen was doing, then sat for a while with my legs idly swinging in the entrance hole, staring off at the purpling shape of a distant range showing low against the far horizon. There were bushes enough up here I reckoned to keep a mule happy for most of the night.

It was fortunate Jeff had been stupid enough to give me this chance to have a good look around, even leaving me the bonus of a torch to do it with. I say 'stupid' because that's just what it was. He didn't know enough about me to have the least basis for such reckless trust. His own sister when she'd hired me out of desperation had put me in the same class as Fletcher and Clampas, a man who lived with a gun. And she had pegged me right. More right than she knew.

Pushing off my perch I dropped into the house Jeff had claimed for his own. It was hard to picture this place as the seat of a community, filled with the noise of a people going about their everyday affairs. They might not have been the ape-men Jeff hunted, or even very close to the beginning of things, but primitive enough to be an unwelcome sight backed into a corner in the dead of night.

I'd a hunch Fern was right in her distrust of this place. I didn't like it either though I couldn't uncover any practical reason. Just a feeling, that was all, a kind of aura that reached out to curl about one. A sense of watchful, breathless waiting as if the place were about to gobble one whole. Damned silly, of course, and I knew it, but knowing didn't chase the feeling away. I went forward again, pulled along by remembrance of that beaded doorway I had seen hunting Flossie.

A thing like that didn't belong in this place. No Indian I had ever brushed up against would have hung a bunch of beads across any doorway. Someone else must taken over this dwelling after the original inhabitants had departed. And if this was the case it had to have been this later group who had so meticulously sealed the place up. Some of Clampas's chindis?

Such bead-hung doorways were not uncommon in Mexican houses.

Thinking of the way this place had been sealed I felt reasonably certain the ones who had been here after the builders had gone must have come and departed many hundreds of years ago. The stillness of centuries hung over these rooms. As I've said, you could feel it.

I switched on the torch and went down the ladder up which Jeff had fetched Flossie.

The pots and bowls still sat where we'd left them and I moved on through three rooms to stop and stare at the preposterous sight of that bead-hung doorway.

The vastness of this quiet seemed to hover

just beyond me in those jet-black shadows retreating before my light, before the sound of each step. I was tense with excitement, with a feverish anticipation and with the prickling dread with which we face the unknown. I kept telling myself there was nothing to be afraid of and, trying to bolster this belief, wouldn't let my hand touch the pistol at my hip.

With the torch aimed dead ahead of me I pushed through the beads with a muttered oath. No one grabbed me. I was faced with nothing but an empty room with a floor hole black before the left-hand wall.

I limped back and got the ladder.

Dropping the heavy end of it through the hole I climbed cautiously down to get off it onto a lower floor which offered little reward for the effort it had taken. A couple of moth-eaten goatskins lay in one corner beside a crude wooden flute. And a handful of pebbles that shone blue in the light.

A few more of these lay scattered this side of the archway giving onto the next room as though dropped in hurried flight or fallen from a burst sack in someone's clumsy fist.

Picking a couple of them up I gave them a closer look. Turquoise nuggets. Good but not gem-grade. All right for beads. I strode on through the arch and stopped with caught breath.

CHAPTER FOURTEEN

The sun was close to two hours high before sounds on the trail below warned that someone at last was approaching from the camp. With a frowning impatience I looked down from the cliff to see Jeff, Fern, Harry and Clampas riding toward the rockfall and, strung out behind them, Jones with six laden packhorses.

I collected Gretchen, flung on my saddle and headed in the same direction, busting to know what the hell they were up to.

When I reached the top of the rockfall the cavalcade below was just coming up to the trailside end of it. Harry, spying me, flung up a hand. "Come down here, Corrigan!" he called like he owned me.

If Gretchen hadn't been all night without water I might have ignored him. In the end with clamped jaws I sent the mule into that jumble of rocks and, sitting back like I was Lord of the Mountain, let her pick her way through them. We came out into the trail and I fastened my stare on a pale-faced Jeff. "What's the idea? You shiftin' camp?"

Jeff looked sick, Hatcher angry, Clampas amused, and Fern about ready to throw in the sponge. "Crew slipped away during the night with that goddam Navajo and better'n half our tinned stuff!" Harry snarled like he eyed it as a personal affront.

"I don't guess he left my Remington, did he?"

Hatcher snorted. "Clampas—who was supposed to be on guard—fell asleep! It's a goddam wonder we didn't all get our throats cut!"

"So we're moving camp," Jeff said tiredly. "I thought if we set up atop that cliff we'd be in a position to keep our eyes on things—"

"And what did you figure to do for water? Pipe it up there?"

Jeff looked embarrassed. "We hadn't thought of that," Fern said.

"You better think of it now." I directed some of my irritation at Clampas. "Why didn't you tell them they'd be killing half the horses trying to get 'em through those rocks?"

Clampas shrugged. "Harry ain't partial to advice from hired hands."

"I can see that," I said. "It's about time

someone told Harry where to head in at. Any kid just out of diapers could have made a better job of this than he has." Catching hold of my temper I told Jeff bluntly, "If I was in charge of this I'd damn quick show Harry where he belongs—at the foot of the line, stripped of all authority."

I saw Larrimore wince, but Fern coming to life said approvingly, "You *are* in charge."

"You can't do this to me!" Harry shouted. "I got a contract with you!"

"Not any longer," I said. "It's been canceled. From here on out you're just one of the hands. And if that doesn't suit, you can spin your bronc an' light a shuck out of here."

Spluttering, frothing, Hatcher was so pissed off he couldn't get a word out. He finally slammed a hand at his gun. Then let go of it like it had scorched him when he found himself staring into mine. I said, "You brought Fletch into this. Now get up there and bury him!"

I watched the man fling out of his saddle and go stomping off to the packs for a shovel. "If I were you," Clampas said with his glance gone solemn, "I'd keep a spare set of eyes in the back of my head."

The Larrimore Expedition was now reduced to a party of six. Knowing the risks of trying to get flatland horses onto the clifftop through that jumble of rocks, I'd have sent the whole lot of them back to the pool had Fern not volunteered to see to their water needs. "I'm afraid it will take up most of your time, Fern."

"Oh, I'm used to commuting. One of the primest facts of life in Chicago. Don't look at me that way—I'll be all right. Don't you think you were just a bit rough on Harry?"

"Man's a born schemer; you should never have employed him."

"I didn't employ him!" she came back angrily. "He was Jeff's idea." Then, more quietly, "You have to realize my brother has little experience outside of the classroom. Most of his life has been devoted to archaeology. After trying for years to get a full professorship he hoped, coming here, to uncover new facts of indisputable significance, credit for which no other scientist would be able to minimize or take away from him." There was a pleading in the smile she tried so desperately to show me. "He knows nothing at all about people like Harry."

"I can understand that."

"Can you understand what he's been hoping to accomplish? Our earliest ancestor, Mousterian Man, has an accepted existence of approximately sixty thousand years, a nomad cropping up in many and diverse places. Now these Basketmaker people of the Anasazi are generally believed to have come into this region some twenty-five thousands of years ago. What Harry hoped to do—and *will* do if he can come up with sufficient evidence—is to connect these two up. Don't you think that's worth doing?"

"I'm just an ignorant country boy, Fern. I wouldn't know up from down about such things."

Jeff, coming over to us, said impatiently, "Hadn't we better get up there, Corrigan?"

I nodded, still choused around in my mind by Fern's pitch. All that kind of guff was so much ancient history, I couldn't see how it could matter today. It was today I'd stuck my neck out to deal with, a time full of danger I could easily recognize. I knew a lot more about what lay ahead of him than Jeff did, and what I knew he wasn't going to like. "Who do you want up there for a helper?"

"Oh, Clampas, I guess. He was certainly a help getting us into this place."

You couldn't fault that. "All right. Take

him up with you. I'll be along soon's I've tended to Gretchen."

I would rather have had Jones. Not so smart but reliable.

When I caught up with them Jeff and his helper had just got as far as the room with the pots he'd had to carry Flossie up from. The pair of them were standing there peering at that collection of relics. I was forced to decide quickly which figured to be the lesser of two tough choices, and said, "Why not start right here?"

"But I told you yesterday," Jeff remarked with surprise, "I'd prefer to go over the whole area before attempting to evaluate anything."

"You're the boss," I nodded, and to Clampas, "Better fetch that ladder along."

"I can see"—Clampas grinned—"you're not one to overlook the natural advantages."

"You look strong enough to carry it," I said, motioning him on after Larrimore.

Each of the empty rooms we went through appeared to deepen the gloom that showed so plain on Jeff's face. "What happened," I said, "to that Mousterian tribe?"

He looked at me in some astonishment; then, catching on, said, "I guess Fern's been talking shop. As a matter of fact there are a number of theories but no substantive evidence."

"Just disappeared like our Basketmakers?"

"That's about the size of it."

The bead curtain now was just ahead of us. Both men stopped to stare, neither liking it. Clampas's eyes jumped at it. "What's that thing doin' here?"

Jeff looked appalled, licked his lips like he couldn't believe it. "Someone's been here. . . ."

"Not since that entrance was sealed," Clampas objected.

"The people who built this never added that touch. Someone's been in here since the builders departed."

"You reckon they cleaned the place out?"

"I don't know," Jeff said bitterly, "but even if I find it the evidence I'm hunting will be open to doubt. Who's going to say now when and how it came to be here? Not with two sets of people running in and out of here."

"Maybe," I said, "we better hunt another site."

"No time for that now," Jeff said miserably. "Might as well get on with it."

He pushed through the dangling strings and stopped, much as I'd done, eyes going to the goatskins and the scattered beads. "Harry"—smiled Clampas—"will be happy to see those."

"Harry," I said, "has pretty well lost whatever edge he was countin' on."

Clampas's glance twinkled amusement. "Time will tell," he said blandly.

"Take this," I told Jeff, handing over Fletch's pistol. "You may find a use for it."

"That's right," Clampas nodded. "Place like this, who can say what might happen?"

"I can tell you what won't," I said. "None of this turquoise is going to wind up with Harry!"

Clampas looked at me and shrugged. Jeff, walking into the next room, swore. Clampas hurried after him and I went in on Clampas's heels. "Jumpin' Jehoshaphat!" Harry's gun-fighter cried. "Looks like the hideout of the Forty Thieves!"

It did indeed. A great assemblage of pots and relics—Jeff called them artifacts—was heaped about the walls in astonishing profusion. One two-foot jar of the storage variety was filled with a miscellany of spear points and arrowheads.

Several others of equal dimensions—as I'd

already discovered—were filled with rough spiderweb turquoise. Eight others were filled with strung beads, also turquoise. Quivers of arrows. A considerable pile of bows of divers styles and vintage were piled alongside. There were hide shields and wooden spears, scrapers, metates and forty-eleven other items too varied to enumerate.

I noticed Jeff staring at something he'd picked up and Clampas, ogling those jars of sky-blue stones, chucked a wink at me with an enchanted grin. "I ain't no authority," he declared with a chuckle, "but what we've got here oughta easily ransom any king those Conquistadores managed to overlook. Congratulations, Larrimore! Looks like you hit the jackpot."

CHAPTER FIFTEEN

There was such a petulant, resentful twist to Jeff's features, I could almost have felt sorry for him if he hadn't made such a mishmash of things.

"What's that you're holding?" I said to him brusquely, and he dropped into my hand a small stone lamp—leastways that's what he called it. To me it was nothing but a rock with a hollow worn into it and a more or less flat bottom, maybe two inches thick and three in diameter. "Valuable?"

"Hey!" Clampas said. "That looks older than Moses."

"Quite a bit older," Jeff replied with a sigh. "Not that it matters. After being found here its age, like its value, has little significance. With two sets of tenants calling this place home, nothing I discover will be worth a plugged nickel."

"In that case," Clampas hurried to assure him, "you can give me the blue stuff and forget you ever saw it."

"Well, come on," I said, "we might as well get on with it. We've still got a couple dozen rooms to get through."

"Sounds like Christmas," Clampas chuckled, giving his hands a promotional dry wash.

Jeff gave him one hard look and thereafter ignored him. He set off for the next room in line, but instead of discarding that 'worthless' stone lamp I noticed it went into his brush jacket pocket.

Any freebooter would have found in this trek through the cliff house a quite ample compensation for the time expended. The next eight rooms provided three motheaten goatskins, a discarded wooden flute, a scatter of mixed black and white beads, three broken pots, an elegant pitcher with a broken snout, three bundles of corn shucks and not another thing.

Jeff sent Clampas back for the ladder.

When the gunfighter returned with it we canvassed two additional rooms, both empty. The first of these, however, had a hole in the floor, and into this Jeff had Clampas drop the ladder. When the man stood aside Jeff motioned him onto it. Clampas looked Jeff over with a speculative stare. "You wouldn't be thinkin' of leaving me down there, now, would you?"

Jeff with a grimace motioned him on, stepping onto the ladder as soon as Clampas got off it on the floor below. So there we were, all three of us, in another empty room. As it eventually turned out every room on this level was empty, much to Clampas's disgust. "How much longer am I totin' this thing?" he growled, giving the ladder a slap with his gun hand.

"Till we're through with it," Jeff said. "Now put it down that hole and let's see what's below."

This next level, I'd been thinking, would likely be the last, so after we'd gone down it

I told him to leave the ladder where it was. There were more rooms down here than on any of the upper levels. "How many people," Clampas asked Harry, "do you reckon lived in this place?"

"I'd say about five hundred."

"At one time?"

"Certainly." Jeff produced a wan smile. "To the people using it this place represented a complete community—a town. Each family had a room."

It was plain such an arrangement held little charm for Clampas. The next fourteen rooms we toured held nothing but discarded odds and ends apparently not cherished by those who had abandoned them, except in the fourteenth where Clampas picked up a rather bleached-looking turquoise ring and two bracelets, all of crude workmanship. Dropping the bangles in his pocket Clampas threw the ring away. Jeff, however, retrieved it, saying, "Keepsake."

The fifteenth and last of the rooms on this, the bottom level, turned out to be an eye-opener, extending into the cliff itself for a distance of possibly some forty feet. "Originally," Jeff told us, "this was probably a cliff shelter, in use sporadically for several hundred years before it was hidden behind this building. One would have to do quite a bit of digging to uncover and date the successive layers of use."

We'd been using the torch on the last couple levels and there wasn't much left in it. I said, "We had better vamoose before we find ourselves stumbling around in the dark."

They'd set up camp just below the rockfall and, time we got down there, Fern was just returning from the pool with the last group of horses she had taken to water. When he saw she was back, Jones beat on his washtub and advised us to come and get it. Advice which no one disregarded.

The main course was beef stew supplemented by cornmeal muffins, java and re-fried beans. To all of which they did full justice. "Well, how'd it go?" Harry asked, trying for a show of his old hearty charm. "Find anything worth carting home?"

"Been more'n one bunch living there," Clampas told him. "Jeff looks about ready to blow the whistle."

Jeff said nothing, just picked up his eating tools, stepped over and dropped them in the tub. Fern said with obvious concern, "Didn't you find a thing?"

Jeff put the stone lamp into her hands.

"Why, this is marvelous!" she cried, turning it over and over. "It must be quite the oldest artifact you've ever found."

"It's old enough, all right," he said glumly, "but how do you prove how it got where and when? I can date it. That's not the point. The problem is provenance. How can I indisputably prove it appeared with the builders, not with those who took over after they left?"

She pushed it around through her head, suddenly smiling in a way that lit up her whole face. "Tree rings," she cried. "We can date the building by the age of the timbers—the roof poles, the wood they put into those ceilings."

"Sure." He nodded. "I thought about that. But what if the age of the stone doesn't match? And it probably won't."

"But if the stone should be older than the timbers—"

"You forget. It's the people, the builders, I'm trying to put dates to. With two different groups having used this place, who's to say which of them first had this lamp?" He thrust it back in his pocket with a lugubrious look. "It may even have been found here, and probably was. In which case, being older than this cliff house, it's of no use at all."

"What do we do now?"

"Tomorrow," Jeff said, "I'm going to have another look at certain features I didn't take the time to study properly. Also I've got to decide which of the pots we'll want to take back with us, for we certainly can't spend more than another week here."

"I'll go with you and help," Fern said. "I don't believe we've enough horses to remove very much. We'll have to box any pottery we take . . ."

"Let's have Brice up there with us," Jeff surprised me by saying.

"Maybe," I said, "it would be better to take Jones. He's pretty handy."

I could feel the probe of her swung-around stare. I'd no idea what she felt about me. For my own part I reckoned I'd been seeing a sight too much of her, one reason she was hard for me to talk to. We had nothing in common. She was big-city, long used to things I knew little about, nor wanted to. My sort of life—if she could have had a good look at it—would have appalled her. The men she knew didn't go around strapped to a shooting iron.

"Don't you want to go with us?"

"Not particularly."

Biting her lip she continued to consider

me, almost as though she thought me willfully stupid. Catching hold of my arm she drew me aside. "What is it with you? Don't you know my brother is counting on you?"

"In a way, perhaps—"

"In every way! You saw how things were. Harry running roughshod—why don't you get rid of him?" Her glance sharpened angrily. "I expected when I gave you Harry's job things were going to be different."

I said, "They are different. Giving me that job has made a prime target out of me!"

Having seen how upset she was I probably shouldn't have said that. A startled look came over her face. Then, flushed and furious, she lashed back. "If you're afraid of him—"

"Don't talk like a fool! What's left of this outfit's about ready to explode. With this goddam heat and all that guff about chindis it'll take damn little . . . Point is until we know—and I mean *know*—which of those buggers is throwin' the wrenches . . ."

"It's your job to find out!"

I gave her a hard look and turned away. I hadn't figured right now to bring things to a boil, but if she thought—Ah, to hell with her! Finding Hatcher watching with that sly smirk on his puss I snarled, "Get a horse and a shovel and don't keep me waiting!"

I tossed my saddle on Gretchen, kneed the air from her belly and cinched her tight. She gave me no argument, knowing I was in no mood to be trifled with. I slipped the bit through her teeth and climbed aboard and, picking up my ex-boss, headed for our previous camp.

"What's up?" Harry said and, getting no answer, buttoned his lip.

When we got through the tamarisks I said without beating around no bushes, "If you found it convenient to get rid of a body, what would you do with it?"

Harry's cheeks turned the color of pummeled dough. "I . . . I—"

"Never mind. I reckon I can find it," I said with a curse, and sent Gretchen over to where Jones had had his fires. I got down, kicked the circle of stones aside and put my eye on Hatcher. "Start diggin'."

With a pasty face Harry bent to the task. I could tell by the ease with which the shovel bit into that fire-blackened dirt we had got the right spot. With the sun not yet down it looked like pretty hot work. He didn't have to go far. I could tell when he straightened, looking sick, he had put his shovel on something that yielded. "Careful now, I don't want him dug up. All I want is a look at his face."

"Wh—Who'd you think we're going to find?"

"Hosteen Joe."

Squatting down, having motioned him out of the way, with my hands I brushed back enough of the loose sandy soil to see that the cadaver had been planted face down, to make out the dried blood and powder marks on his shirt. "Shot in the back close up. With a pistol. Turn him over."

Harry's sweat-shiny face was a picture of horror. Shaking like a leaf he drew back in repugnance. "For Chrissake," I said, "he's not goin' to bite you!"

I caught hold of the hair, jerked the head up enough for him to see it was Joe, then let it fall back. "All right. Cover him up."

CHAPTER SIXTEEN

We hadn't much more than got through the tamarisks on the way back to camp when, rounding a bend, we found Clampas riding toward us.

"Ah, the Mule Man and stooge," he

hailed, combing us over with his sardonic look. "Much as we'll regret the loss of your company, if I was you, Harry, I'd trot right along."

Hatcher, with the look of a frightened rabbit, appeared only too glad to be let off the hook.

Clampas's gaunt face swung back to me. "Where the hell you been? They're all out huntin'—figured the chindis had got you."

I just stared at him, not saying anything. He laughed. "So you found him. Kinda figured you would. Takes one to know one." He looked amused. "That Harry," he chuckled. Then his brows drew down. "You don't believe it?"

"He hasn't the stomach for that kind of thing. You were using that smartass buck all along, right from the time he showed up with old Two-Feathers. What'd you promise him—that Sharps? It was you put him up to makin' off with those horses. You probably used him to get rid of the crew."

"Sure. I had to figure some way of cuttin' down the odds." Clampas grinned. "Hell, Fletch was no loss, an' I won't shed no tears if something happens to that mealy-mouthed Harry. You been around. Quit usin' your head for a hat rack. Comes to that, your

166

friend Harry propositioned me two days ago, wanted us to team up and split that turquoise right down the middle!"

I felt an almost overmastering impulse to go after him right then. "Guess you allowed you didn't need his help."

Clampas smiled. "Not likely. If I'd said anything like that he might of taken the notion I aimed to grab it myself."

"I suppose that never entered your mind."

"Oh, I've thought some about it—of course Hatcher doesn't know about that pile we saw this morning. If I was figurin' to team up with anyone it sure wouldn't be with no chump like Harry."

"Guess you'd want a man you could count on."

"Now you're talkin'."

"Don't look at me. I like this layout just the way it is."

"Here," he said, tossing me a penny. "Flip it—I'm going to show you something."

Almost before the coin left my hand Clampas's gun flashed up. It coughed just once and the penny disappeared. "Kid stuff," I said.

I could see he was graveled. "Corrigan," he said, "you amaze me."

"Just be careful that shooter don't point in my direction or you ain't going to care whether school keeps or not."

He didn't like that either. He looked me over for a while before he said, "How's Burt Mossman getting along these days?"

"Haven't seen Burt since I quit the Hash-knife."

"No accountin' for tastes," he said lightly. Then he fetched out that bullypuss smile once more. "Just do yourself a favor and stay out of my way."

Next morning, with the promise of another hot day, I heard Jeff telling Jones to take over Fern's watering chores, that she'd be going with him to decide what relics they wanted out of the cliff house. When Jones turned away to get this work started I led Jeff off a piece and told him bluntly, "You better take Harry up there and leave me in camp."

"I don't want Harry up there."

"It ain't a question of what you want but what you can afford. I don't think you'd be real smart to leave Hatcher and Clampas here with no one to keep an eye on them."

"Not sure I get your point," Jeff said, frowning.

"All right, I'll spell it out. How do you aim to get whatever artifacts you want back to your headquarters in Chicago?"

"I'm intending to use those horses."

"And when you're ready to go suppose there ain't any horses?"

"You think Harry—"

"Harry," I said, "is under Clampas's thumb. He's scared to death of that bucko."

"Why would Clampas want to tamper with our horses?"

"He's already tampered with them once through Harry. You think Clampas was asleep when your crew took off? Wake up, Larrimore. You're dealin' with the *real* world here! Clampas saw that turquoise yesterday, damn near a wagonload, and I'm telling you fair and square he has no intention of seeing it wind up in some university."

"What makes you think—?"

"Hell, he as much as told me. Said Harry had offered to split with him. Be no problem at all to run off those horses and cache them out of sight till you and your sister have started hoofin' it for the railroad."

Jeff stared at me, shaken. "You want me to make them a present of it?"

"All I want you to do is face the facts

and make it no easier for them than you can help."

I watched him go off and beckon Harry. When I swung around there was Fern with a tired look to the set of her shoulders. "So you're not going up with us?"

I shook my head, not wanting to get trapped into another unprofitable argument. But she wouldn't leave it like that. She said, coaxing, "I'd feel a lot safer if—"

"Fern, believe me, it won't do to leave Harry and Clampas down here together."

She kept searching my face with that blue-green stare, the rising sun in her hair like copper. She was not a person easily put off. "Look," I said, "both Harry and Clampas are bustin' to get their hooks on that turquoise. Harry's soft—we can handle him. But Clampas is something else again. He's got no more scruples than a goddam snake."

"You don't have to convince me; I had a feeling about him as soon as I saw him. I told you that. It's why I wanted you to come with us. But I'm just as upset by those rooms up there. I've a very bad feeling about that place every time I step into it. It isn't anything I can easily explain; there's something evil about it, a feeling of menace as though something horrible had taken place there and was waiting—just waiting like a spider in its web—to happen all over again."

She put a hand on my arm and I could feel her tremble with the freckles standing out against the pallor of that tipped-back face as she stood there looking up at me with the need so apparent in those searching eyes. "At least come with us—"

"As I've just pointed out to your brother, if you intend to take anything away from this place you can't afford to lose those horses, Fern. Jeff may not have found what he hoped to but the things he *has* found are commercially valuable, enough to pay for more than one extensive dig. He can't want to throw all that away through losing the means of taking it out of here."

I could see these things weren't touching her at all. I'd been throwing my words against a locked mind, a stubborn conviction it seemed nothing would loosen. What she wanted, I thought, and really needed, was a man of her own, and she had fastened on me.

Her next words proved it. In a voice gone husky, her hand tightening its grip, those near-whispered words banged against me like fists: *"If you care at all for me, Brice . . ."*

I jerked myself free. "It's no good, I tell you! Stay away from me, Fern. I wouldn't fit into your life. Nor you in mine!"

CHAPTER SEVENTEEN

After Fern, her brother and Harry went into the rockfall on their way to the cliff house entrance I sleeved the sweat off my face and looked around for Clampas. Jones was just coming back from a trip to the pool with the first batch of horses he had taken to water. I hailed him to ask if he'd seen the fellow. "Clampas? Sure. He's down at the old camp."

"Doing what?"

Jones said dryly, "I didn't ask." Something in my expression apparently spurred him to say, "You want I should tell him to get his ass up here?"

"No, let it go. What I've got to say to him can wait a while longer."

I rolled me a smoke while he penned the horses he had just brought back and set off for the pool with the rest of our stock. Which reminded me that Gretchen hadn't been watered yet. "You'll just have to wait a bit," I told her. "I ain't about to go off and leave

172

them critters unguarded till I've had me a little chat with that bugger."

God but it was hot. Seemed like each day was even hotter than the last. And by the looks of that sky there was no relief in sight. I felt mean about Fern but it was one of those things you had to nip in the bud, and I reckoned I'd done the right thing if I could stick to it.

I looked around for Flossie and then remembered she'd gone with Fern. I hoped that ladder Jones had put together for us wouldn't decide to come apart while somebody was on it. Seemed like I was working up a fit of the dismals. I wasn't the kind to set around and do nothing. Aside from keeping an eye on the penned horses, which I got to admit was becoming monotonous, what was there to do?

Jones came back with the last of the watered stock and after he'd penned them came over and hunkered down on his bootheels. He picked up a stick and made doodles in the dirt. "When's the professor pullin' out, do you know?"

"Within the week I guess." I shifted my weight. "Clampas still down there?"

Jones nodded. "What happens to us when they get to the railroad?"

I looked up without interest. "Reckon they'll pay us off."

Even in the shade sweat was all over us and the goddam flies wouldn't let us alone. I finally got up and just about then horse sound swiveled our heads toward the trail.

As expected it was Clampas. He swung off his horse with that sardonic grin, stood looking at us with the reins in his hand. "Still up there, are they?"

Neither one of us bothered to answer. With a shrug he went off to put his mount in the pen. "Wonder," I said, "what he was doing down there."

"Wasn't doin' nothing. Just settin' there under them tamarisks."

"Hatchin' up more devilment probably."

He came back after a while and bit himself off a chew from his Picnic Twist. "I see Harry comin' down but no sign of the others."

When I heard Hatcher's boots coming out of the rocks I turned around for a look at him. He wore the shine of sweat on his troubled face. When he got back his breath he said, "I couldn't take no more of it. That's the scariest place I ever been into."

"See any chindis?" Clampas grinned.

"No, but I sure seen a mort of turquoise."

Naked greed gleamed out of his stare. "You reckon he's sure enough aimin' to pack it all back to that fool university?"

"It ain't got there yet," Clampas mentioned, and swiveled his glance for a look at me. I paid him no heed. "Have they made up their minds what stuff they're going to take?" I asked Harry.

"I guess they're takin' six or eight of them pots. And the turquoise." He scowled. "Sure makes me sick to think of it. If we had any gumption we'd take it away from him."

"Watch out," Clampas drawled. "That sort of gab don't set well with Corrigan."

Hatcher eyed me, disgusted.

"When are the Larrimores comin' down?" Jones asked. He slanched a look at the sun. "Mebbe I better wrastle up some grub."

Harry kicked at a horse apple. "Jeff allows he's goin' to spend the night up there."

Clampas chuckled. "Figures to keep his eye on the turquoise, I reckon." He spun the rowel of a spur. "Wouldn't want anything to happen to him. . . . Maybe I ought to go up an' keep him company."

I reckoned he was trying to get a rise out of me.

A shadow crossed my lap. I looked up and saw Fern coming toward us. "Hi," she said,

175

flushed of face and looking straight at me. "Hi," I said. "That right about Jeff? He's really fixin' to stay up there?"

"That's what he says. He wants Jones to fetch him some food and a water bag when it's ready."

Harry said, "I wouldn't spend a night in that place for all the gold in the Denver mint!" And Clampas said solemnly, "Ain't likely, Harry, they'll offer it to you."

After we'd eaten, Jones with a water bag slung from his shoulder took a pan heaped with grub and set out for the cliff house. Fern said to me with an expressionless face, "You meant that, didn't you?"

"Yes. Where's the dog?" I saw the whole shape of her stiffen, but whatever she felt it wasn't being advertised. I thought for a moment the breath had caught in her throat; her eyes never left my face as she replied, "She's staying up there with Jeff."

It seemed to be awful quiet for a second. Then she turned, moved away toward her tent, and I found Clampas watching from between the two pens Jones had put the horses into. In an effort to put Fern's look out of mind I walked up to him grimly and stared him in the eye. "You're not going to get it, Clampas. Make up your mind to it.

And if anything should happen again to what's left of our remuda you can look for big trouble."

Jeff was back in time for breakfast. Flossie, too; and the first thing she did was make a beeline for Fern's tent. When Fern came out with her a few minutes later it was with her usual calmly competent appearance despite the dark smudges I saw under her eyes.

After we'd eaten Jeff drew me aside and speaking under his breath said, "There was something up there—must have been about four o'clock. I'd been dozing I guess and had forgot to turn off my torch. It was pretty weak when I jerked open my eyes and saw this shape slipping out of the room. Just as it seemed about to fade through that arch I yelled. The top part of it turned and I was staring at the most terrifying face I've ever seen in my life. Great ringed eyes beneath fluttering tatters of ropelike hair, and a leering mouth parted over two teeth behind lips that must have been at least an inch thick."

"Sure you weren't dreaming?"

"I wish I could think so, but when I saw that horrible face peering at me I was wide awake. Believe me I was! I can see it now, grinning around those two teeth!" He swallowed convulsively. "You think it was a chindi?"

Some of what he felt must have rubbed off on me. The sweat grew cold on the back of my neck. I stood motionless, not answering, trying to control leaping thoughts, my eyes fastened on Clampas. "No," I said, looking again at Jeff, "I think you saw an illusion—"

"Damn it," he growled. "I *saw* it, I tell you!"

"Of course. I'm sure you did. I'll stay up there tonight and see if I can catch a glimpse. Were you in that room with all those jugs of turquoise at the time this happened?"

Jeff nodded. "I was trying to make up my mind how much of it we could pack."

"All right," I said. "Keep your mouth shut about this," and limped off to saddle Gretchen.

Riding up through the rockfall I left the mule outside the cliff house entrance, wriggled my way through the hole we had made and set off to find if there was anything I could discover. Like, for instance, if there was some other way of getting into the place. I figured Jeff had been too shaken to make any kind of thorough hunt himself. Of course we'd already canvassed the place but I had an idea I wanted to check out.

Down the ladder I went and into the room where we'd found the first pots. Jeff had separated a few of these and set them to one side, possibly the ones he was figuring on taking. He'd fetched up and put with these that pitcher with the broken snout. I hadn't thought to bring a torch so there wasn't much point in going stumbling about through the dark of those lower rooms scratching matches to see with.

This being the level with the occasional apertures left in the outside wall for windows, I was about to head for that room behind the strings of beads when a swift patter of feet wheeled me around to see Flossie happily wagging her tail in the doorway behind me. "Where's Fern?" I said, and Fern answered for herself, coming to stand beside the dog and holding out a torch. She said, a bit uncertain-like, "I came up to fetch this for you. Didn't think you could do very much without a light."

"Too right," I said. "I tore off in such a hurry I forgot to bring one with me."

I expect I felt more awkward than she did, remembering the things we had said to each other. "If—if you'd like to come along, I want to check on that turquoise . . ."

"If I won't be in the way."

"You carry the torch," I said, watching Flossie scamper eagerly ahead of us.

Still with an occasional window hole lighting the way, we came to and pushed through that bead-hung doorway and came into the room with the pair of old goatskins where a handful of turquoise had lain scattered on the floor. "We picked that up yesterday," Fern said, and we moved on through the arch, stepping into the room where we'd found what Clampas had termed the "chindis' hoard." There were changes here too.

"We picked out what we thought was the best of it and piled it over there," she said, pointing. "Neither one of us, however, knows hardly anything about turquoise. We'd be obliged if you'd go through it and weed out the ordinary stuff. It's going to be a real weight problem taking very much of it, I'm afraid."

"If we all went on foot you'd have six more horses you could pack," I pointed out. "And if you don't take it out—all of it, I mean—by the time you're able to return somebody else will have scooped it up."

She looked at me tiredly. "I guess you mean Harry and Clampas."

"You bet. One of them anyway. When's Jeff figurin' to leave?"

"He says tomorrow." She sighed. "I don't think we can be ready by tomorrow. Too much to pack up and all that carrying down through the rockfall. I dread to think of it."

"Speaking of dread," I said, taking a look at her, "do you still have that feeling about this place?"

"Yes. More than ever. I'll be glad to see the last of it."

"I remember you thought something terrible must have happened here, that these rooms were waiting for it to happen again."

"Yes." She shivered. "I still feel that way."

"I've had a few uncomfortable thoughts about the place myself. There's a brooding, sinister sort of atmosphere I find it hard to explain away. More than just this tomblike quiet. It's as though the very mud and stones have soaked up the horror and anguish—"

"Don't talk about it, Brice. I'm just about ready to scream right now."

She looked it, too.

"All right. Let's go—where's Flossie?"

Fern whistled. Away off somewhere down

below a dog barked. "Here, Flossie!" Fern called, and the dog barked again. "She's on a lower level," I said. "Stay here. I'll fetch the ladder."

"I'm coming with you," she said, hurrying after me.

I hooked the ladder over my shoulder and we started back. When we got to the hole I dropped the ladder into position. "Throw some light down there." When she did we saw Flossie, tail wagging and looking proud as Punch with a long bone sticking out from both sides of her mouth. I said, "Good girl, Flossie," and to Fern: "How will we get her up? Can you carry her?"

"I don't think so, not and climb that ladder. She's pretty heavy. I better get Jeff."

I said irritably, "You'll have to have the ladder to get onto the next floor." With exasperation mounting, I hauled up the ladder and manhandled it back where I'd got it. When it was in position she said, "You keep this," and handed me the switched-off torch.

The sun coming through those window holes made it plain it would soon be dropping out of sight. In this kind of country black night wouldn't be long delayed. It was odd we hadn't found any Indian-made ladders. By the time I'd quit wondering about this I was back in the room above Flossie so I switched on the torch and there she was, still chomping that old bone she'd dug up.

With the torch still on I remembered the notion that had fetched me up here. Squatting down put me under the sun glare coming in from outside and I switched off the torch, juggling that notion around and thinking it had to be sound. Because, unless Jeff's apparition turned out to be a permanent resident, it someway had to get in from outside, and the only feasible way it could do this was through one of these top-level window holes. And that meant a rope with an anchor at one end of it.

Why not, I thought, go and look for it now? There ought to be time before Fern brought Jeff up here. I shoved to my feet and walked into the next room—nothing there, nor in any of the others on this level until I remembered I hadn't thought to check the three rooms on the downtrail side of that bead curtain.

Well, I expect you guessed it. Our chindi had climbed into the turquoise room; there was the rope coming in across the sill of the window hole, held in place by the metal bar it was tied to—only, by grab, it was no metal bar but the dismantled barrel of my given-away Remington!

CHAPTER EIGHTEEN

Jeff went down and brought up Flossie, bone and all. He did not appear too happy about it; I expect he felt considerable put out, dragooned into playing errand boy to a dog. Flossie fetched her bone over for Fern to admire and was visibly delighted by Fern's lavish praise.

Jeff, looking at me, said, "You want to check this turquoise for me? Seems to be all I'll have to show for this trip."

"You've got that Stone Age lamp in your pocket."

"Well, yes," he nodded, "but I can't tie it in to what I came here for. Offhand, how much of this mineral would you say is worth moving?"

"Offhand, I'd say all of it. And by walking the forty miles between here and the railroad you'll have enough horses to tote it. You've got a king's ransom here if you can manage to get out with it."

"I hope you know what you're talking about," he muttered, perking up a little.

This was my hope, too, but getting it to Chicago was like to take a heap of doing.

It was just about then I saw him suddenly stiffen, startled stare clamped intent on the bone Flossie was gnawing. "Here—let me see that," he grunted, bending over.

Flossie growled, backing off.

"Let me have a look at that," Jeff said warily. And Fern said, "He isn't going to keep it. Here—let me have it."

The dog, distrustfully dancing about, reluctantly surrendered her coveted prize.

Peering over his shoulder I said, "Doesn't much look like it came off a steer."

Looking immensely excited, Jeff looked up to say, "It's a human leg bone, what there is of it. I'll have to get it dated, but near as I can tell it's about the same age as that stone lamp I found."

"Good girl!" Fern told Flossie. "Let's go find another, shall we?"

Flossie, thus encouraged, straightaway leaped to the floor below and was off like a bat out of Carlsbad. "Come on!" Jeff cried, and went hurrying down our makeshift ladder. With a deal more care Fern and I followed. But the dog was no longer on that level. "She's making for that cave shelter," Jeff declared excitedly.

When we reached it Flossie, half out of sight, was making the dirt fly. In less than two minutes she came scrambling out with another aged bone, an arm bone this was, and Jeff looked even more excited than she was.

Peering into the excavation with the aid of the torch we could see a number of other half-buried bones and the lower two thirds of a badly smashed skull.

Fern, looking sick, backed hastily away. Eyes bright, Jeff said, "I'll have to get a shovel—"

I caught hold of his arm. "We forgot to fetch the ladder."

But there was no holding Jeff. "Wait here," he growled, and took off at a run. Looked like Flossie's find had made a new man of him.

Fern, I could see, did not share his enthusiasm. With waxen cheeks and worried stare she followed me into the part of the room that was not under the fire-blackened overhang. Recalling the look of that smashed skull I couldn't help wondering how many other mangled bodies had been buried here. Fern tried to get Flossie to leave the bone alone but, having been robbed once, the dog had no intention of giving up this newest prize.

My thoughts shifted to the man who had climbed that rope with the aid of my dismantled Remington, a dangerous feat exposed as he must have been against that sheer wall. He could not be seen from our present camp but he risked at the least a very nasty fall in the event the rope broke or any portion of that wall collapsed. Was this the man with the horrible face described by Jeff?

I reckoned Jeff was into the rockfall by this time. Even without the ladder, getting out of this place offered no great problem; I had done it myself without any ladder. Be different of course for Fern and the dog.

In the creeping breathless quiet the sound of approaching steps carried plainly and Clampas came into our caveshelter room on the heels of Jeff and the shovel he'd gone after. I could see Flossie bristle. Clampas reached for the shovel. "Just show me where and I'll do the digging. Expect you've already seen all we're likely to find."

But he was wrong about that. In little more than half an hour's work he uncovered six skeletons, not counting Flossie's find, and the heads of each had been smashed like the first. "Looks like they been poleaxed," he said. "No jewelry. You want to clear any more?"

"I guess we've seen enough," Jeff allowed. "We better get back to camp. You all right, Fern?"

"I've felt better."

Jeff picked up the shovel. Flossie picked up her bone and hustled after Fern.

"Don't you think," Fern said, catching her brother's arm, "we ought to cover them up?"

"They're not goin' to object," Clampas said. "But here's the shovel if you don't feel right about it."

By the time they'd moved the ladder twice and twice lifted Flossie onto the next level, Jeff's feeling that all was well with his world looked to have dampened down somewhat. The sun was nearing the horizon when we came out on the clifftop and Fern, Flossie and Jeff up ahead were again debating their time of departure. Clampas, several yards behind, showed a mocking smile when I caught up on my faithful steed.

"You're goin' to wear that goddam mule to a frazzle if you ain't careful," he said.

"She paces herself—got more sense than a horse," I told him. "I been wonderin' about the way Fletch was killed—with that dart, I mean. You got any idea where it came from?"

"Hell," Clampas said, "I just retched up an' jabbed the thing into him."

"I wouldn't put it past you."

Clampas looked amused. "Come off it, Corrigan. You must think I'm some kinda one-man exterminator."

"Jeff had a bit of excitement last night. While he was up there sleeping with that turquoise some cat-footed jasper in a ceremonial mask slipped into the room trying to give him a fright."

"That so? Was he frightened?"

"Reckon it startled him some. They're not used to chindis in Chicago. I gave him Fletch's six-shooter, told him next time he sees one to salivate the bastard."

Clampas laughed. "By the way," he said, "didn't it strike you as odd there wasn't no jewelry on them guys we dug up?"

"I doubt if them Basketmakers wore any gewgaws. If they did they were probably stripped before they were planted." We went along a few mule lengths without any more chitchat. Then I said to him casual, "I'll be staying up there tonight. Happen you run into that venturesome chindi you can tell him he needn't risk his neck on that rope.

I'll leave the door off the latch and he can walk right in like he's one of the family."

We went down through the rockfall and put on the nosebags.

After we finished feeding our tapeworms, and I got back from getting Gretchen a drink at the pool, Fern waylaid me before I could start once more for the cliff house.

"Do you feel you really have to spend another night up there? Why don't you just forget that turquoise—surely you can't believe it's worth such a risk. Now that Flossie has discovered those bones . . ."

"Those bones," I said, "if they pack the right date, might well put Jeff where he's achin' to be, right up at the top of the archaeological totem pole. And if he can get that turquoise back to Chicago he can be almost certain of coming back here next year; no one could afford to stand in his way."

"But why should—Brice, why should you care whether he comes back or not? I'm afraid of that place. I don't think you ought to stay up there—it's dangerous!"

"Aren't you forgetting? Danger's my business, my stock in trade. As for carin' whether or not your brother comes back . . . hell,

I'm countin' on him hiring me at double my present wages."

I endured a long look, hoping she wouldn't bawl. With the orneriest grin I was able to dredge up I pointed Gretchen into the rockfall, still feeling the drag of her stare on my back.

At the cliff house entrance I pulled my bridle and tack off the mule and turned her loose to forage for herself, pretty sure she'd come running if she heard me call. Then I went inside, picked up Fern's torch, went down the ladder onto the next level and listened to the rasp of my spurless boots stalking through the piled-up silence of centuries. I had the same creepy feel the place had given me the first time, but I was no silly girl to let it build fantastic fancies.

Reaching the turquoise room I limped across to the window hole, pulled up that rope and untied it from the barrel of my stockless Remington. The barrel had some fresh scratches but near as I could tell no further damage. I guessed it would still shoot and made sure that it was loaded, taking out the cartridges and dropping them in my pocket. Then I took the barrel with its still workable mechanism into the next room and laid it down in a corner where I hoped it wouldn't be noticed.

I got the rope then and tossed it down onto the floor below, not caring to give Clampas's chindi the least bit of aid I was able to avoid. With this same thought in mind I went back and removed the ladder from where it had rested against the floor above. Now, I reckoned, chindis or not they could hardly drop in without me hearing them. But just to make sure, I moved back out of sight and sat down on the floor with my back to a wall below the hole I'd just taken the ladder from.

After my recent talk with Harry's gunfighter I was not at all sure I would have any visitors. I didn't think Clampas would intrude on my vigil. Dangerous he was, I'd no doubt about that, but men of his stamp preferred the odds to be with them. They didn't like going up against a pat hand.

I was a long way from making up my mind about Harry. I had him figured for a slick-talking con man and all I had seen of him bore this out. Ruthless enough with things going his way, but when push came to shove he had twice backed off. And he had certainly appeared to be afraid of this place. Had this all been an act? Was he at rock bottom a lot tougher than he looked? Appearances for sure could be almighty deceptive.

It seemed three times as quiet now as it had when I came in here. The same breathless hush that had raised my hackles before, the same sense of unspeakable evil Fern had felt to be cooped up in these ancient walls seemed abruptly less than a hand's grab away.

I advised me not to let myself run away with any such preposterous notion but it did not take the curse from this quiet that seemed to be soaking right into my bones. Outside in the heat of a blazing sun a man could scoff at such nonsense, but as the cold of the night settled into these rooms nothing appeared too outlandish to seem possible. Not even chindis.

I would have liked to have had my pistol in hand but was too keyed up now to risk the least movement. Twice I thought to have heard a stealthy foot; once I'd have sworn I'd caught the slither of cloth brushing unseen against something in passing.

I was fast becoming a bundle of nerves.

With no idea how long I'd been rooted there with muscles cramped and ears about ready to fall off with listening it took a real effort to get off my behind. Every joint in my body was stiff with cramp, so locked in position I fully expected to hear them creak with the strain. But eventually, by degrees, I got onto my feet, feeling like I had been dragged through a knothole.

The place was as still as the night before Christmas, and if anything was stirring I sure didn't hear it. When I felt I could move without breaking apart I crept into the next room and over to the window hole for a look at the night. The moon had got up, but although not in sight the argent gleam of its presence lay wraithlike along the opposite wall of the gulch.

Pulling off my boots to cut down the racket, I slipped through the bead strings and over to the door hole that let into the room where the king's ransom lay. Someone a long time ago had assembled it there and never come back for it.

Would Jeff's luck be any better? I wondered.

CHAPTER NINETEEN

It must have been pretty well along toward morning when I got to remembering my days on the trading post at Half Step. I didn't think of them often. Growing up as a kid, every day had been an adventure—learning to ride and seeing new faces, getting to know a lot of interesting Indians, admiring the jewelry they brought in to trade or leave as pawn when they ran short of cash. But when I reached my teens this was all old stuff and hanging around that place bored the hell out of me and going off to school, after the first couple of years, seemed just as bad. I was probably fiddle-footed. What I wanted was excitement and I found it with Burt Mossman. He had the coldest eye I have ever looked into. . . .

Of a sudden I found myself bolt upright, listening into that brooding silence, staring wide-eyed into the dark around. Something, I thought, had shifted its weight. But what? And where?

Motionless, listening, I snapped on my torch, aiming it into the black hole of that doorway, thinking to see a faint blur of motion. I couldn't pick it up; the light was too nearly spent to give any definition. I lunged to my feet and tore into the room where the two goatskins lay and found nothing but shadows that drifted away in the fading dimness of my torch. All I could hear was a wild thudding inside me. Then a sound like a fast freight car passing and something whacked into the wall behind me and I threw the damn torch in a passion of cursing. No grunt or cry came out of the shadows, nothing but the clatter of the rolling torch.

Strangely enough as I crouched there panting I had a vision of that dart in Fletcher's throat and sensed it must have been sped from an ordinary peashooter. And there was nobody near me and I knew for sure that except for myself this room was empty. No one had left by that moonlit window hole.

I pulled in a fresh breath and straightened out of my cramp. I turned back to the doorway. I'd come through so reckless and felt along the wall but there was no dart there. What I jerked from the wall was a feathered arrow.

It was getting light fast with the night all but gone when I limped back to cautiously examine the window hole. No rope nor any mark of one. What the lift of my stare discovered outside was a deal more startling. Spread along the rim of the gulch wall opposite were the motionless shapes of a long line of horsemen, black against the brightening sky.

Indians!

I tore out of that room through the dangling beads and through three more and straight up the ladder and squeezed through the holes we had made getting in here and out on the clifftop and, not stopping for breath, flung my saddle on Gretchen and took off for camp.

Only Jones was afoot, building up his fire, when I went down through the rockfall in a clatter of hoofs with six-shooter lifted, belching out the alarm. "Indians!" I yelled, pulling up by the fire in a splatter of dust. "Not two miles away—must be half a hundred of 'em!"

Clampas and Harry came running with rifles and Fern and Flossie tumbled out of their tent just as Jeff appeared, struggling into his shirt. "Where?" Harry cried with eyes so bulged I thought they'd roll off his cheekbones.

"They were on that wall across from the cliff house—"

"But there's no place to hide! We'll be slaughtered like sheep!" Harry jittered.

"Not if you can get yourselves into the cliff house."

"But the horses!" Jeff wailed. "They'll—"

"Hell with the horses!" To get them moving, knowing better, I snarled, "If you don't want to find yourselves over a fire, for Chrissake get out of here! Pronto!"

"Too late," Jones muttered, throwing out a pointing arm.

I wheeled. He was right. Whatever the outcome we were trapped here now. Both cliffs were black with jostling horsemen. Spears, bows and miscellany of rifles were plainly visible as were many of the faces. Navajos, all of them, and not to be trifled with.

Now, on the opposite wall, the ranks opened up and a commanding figure put his pony down the precipitous slope on skidding hind legs to pull to a stop less than twenty feet away. The vicious slam of a shot ripped the sudden silence and I whirled to find Harry staggering backward off balance. Clampas, his face gaunt, had wrenched the rifle from Hatcher's grasp and thrown it into the brush. The Navajo—it was old Johnny Two-Feathers—sat his mount imperturbably, making no move at all.

"I will talk," he said, "with Man-on-a-Mule."

"Go ahead. I'm listening."

"This is bad thing you do. Going into the house of the Anasazi, stirring up the chindis. Taking away things that do not belong to you. Bring very bad trouble."

He studied me awhile. "Where Hosteen Joe?"

A very sticky question.

"Dead," I said finally.

"So," the old man smiled thinly. "You admit it."

"I don't think you'd care for a lie."

"Where?"

I said, "Matter of fact we thought he'd gone off with the boys who deserted our crew one night . . ."

"We talk with crew. Joe not with them."

I could see what was coming, but no way around it.

"You show," he said.

"Joe's at the old camp. By the tamarisks."

Johnny Two-Feathers nodded.

"Come," he said. "You show."

I could feel the sweat trickle down my back. But there was no way around it, not without blood shed, and most of the blood would damn sure be ours.

"All right." I put Gretchen onto the trail and the old man swung his horse in behind. A grim and talkless ride. Some awful thoughts churned through my head, but nothing I could dredge up offered so much as the faintest glimmer of any way out of this.

I put Gretchen through the trees. The old man on his horse came through behind me. "Where?" he said. "Where you put Joe?"

It was plain no explanation I might make could wash away the fact of that bullet through Joe's back. "I should have fetched a shovel."

He waved that away. I pointed out the place, thinking maybe he wasn't minded to have Joe disturbed, a forlorn hope that didn't last any longer than it took him to walk over there. He shoved away the stones, began scuffing at the soft dirt under them.

When he was down about a foot he got onto his knees and began scooping the dirt out with his hands. It didn't take long before Joe's shirt came into view with the dried blood still showing. The old man stared a long while at that sight without opening his mouth.

When he presently got up he considered me grimly.

"Who shoot Joe?"

So I told him how I'd wondered if after all, as we'd supposed, Joe had really ridden off with our crew, and how I'd come down here on a hunch to have a look. And found him. Not putting any name to the man who'd come with me.

But I could see straightaway it wasn't going to be enough. Still holding me with that bitter bright stare, "Who shoot Joe?" he said again.

"I wasn't there—how could I know?"

That bleak brown stare stayed on my face for an interminable while, then abruptly he said, "Paleface say one eye for an eye. You no tell I pick someone. Navajo have roast brain for breakfast." With a teeth-showing scowl he climbed back on his pony and rode through the trees.

It looked like Larrimore's ill-fated expedition was in for more trouble than it could happily stomach. If I didn't divulge my suspicions of Clampas . . . It just wasn't in me to play that game. I could, without regret or compunction, kill that devil if it came to a showdown, but turn him over to be tortured by these Indians I simply couldn't do, even though I'd Two-Feathers's word somebody was going to have to pay for Joe's murder.

When we came once again into a camp gone silent as that damned cliff house, the old man, staring like a graven image on his piebald pony, held up both arms and wasted few words. "A young Navajo man has been killed at your campfire. The People have suffered much and long from the white man's duplicity. You will take nothing from this house of the Anasazi. You have until sunrise tomorrow to give up man who kill Hosteen Joe. I have spoken."

With no more talk he drove his colorful mount up the opposite slope.

You can imagine the result of those remarks once he'd gone. The stupid uproar, the fright and the bluster, everyone trying to shout down the others. When I'd heard enough of it I said sharply, "If we refuse to dredge up a sacrifice for him he'll do the picking. This camp is not defensible. We're sitting ducks."

"Why don't you do something?" Harry demanded of me, and there were nods all around; the only dissensions being Flossie and Fern.

"I intend to," I said. "Soon as it's dark I'm going up to the cliff house and if the rest of you want to stay alive a little longer you'll do the same. Up there, until we run out of ammunition we can probably hold them off."

"And what about our horses?"

"The Navajos have gone," Hatcher cried. "I say let's make a run for it!"

"They haven't gone. They've only dropped out of sight. There's no way they'll be leaving this place till they've got what they came after. They'll be satisfied with that and our empty-handed departure. But you try to slip out of here and you'll be dead before you've gone a half mile."

"We ain't givin' nobody up!" Harry howled.

"They're not after you." Clampas grinned. "I'll lay you forty to one it's the—"

"Shut your damn trap!" I snarled at him, but Fern had already sensed it was her they'd demand. "Put it to a vote," Jones suggested, and I nodded. "All those in favor of letting them have Fern—if that's who they ask for—stick up your hands."

Harry's hand went up like a shot. No one else moved, but the look in their eyes showed what they thought of him. Clampas said, "Corrigan should have told that Injun it was you killed Joe."

Jeff came enough out of his trance to want to be told where the cavalry was, and Clampas laughed. "Settin' around in their friggin' barracks, of course." He threw a look at me. "Sure goes against my grain to pull out of this place without them stones the chindis been hoardin'."

"Surely," Jeff said, trying to pull himself together, "some of us could break through if we made a concerted rush for it?"

"You're welcome to try," I said dryly. "It's going to cost them something to lift my scalp." I looked them over once more. "If the one who killed Joe doesn't give himself up there ain't one of us going to leave here alive."

As soon as it got dark enough to hide our movements we slipped one by one into that jumble of fallen rocks to make our attempt to get into the dubious safety of the cliff house. Each moment of that climb I expected to hear or feel the slap of a bullet and had little doubt the others felt likewise. We were fetching what stores we were able to carry. Way it turned out none of us had thought to bring up any wood. I had purely hated to leave Gretchen behind, but in the interest of harmony had turned her loose without saddle or bridle to fend for herself.

It was a nerve-racking climb but we got to the top of the cliff without incident. Flossie, eager as always, was the first one in. Lathered with impatience the rest of us wriggled our way through the entrance Jones and Clampas had opened, though not in some cases without second thoughts.

Fern and I were the last ones in and she said, voice husky, "I'd give a good deal to be somewhere else. Do you think we've any chance of ever getting out of this?"

"Do you know if anyone thought to fetch a torch?"

"I brought one. I think Clampas fetched two. You haven't answered my question."

"The probabilities are self-evident. Even," I said, "if by some sort of miracle we do manage to get clear, it doesn't seem a heap likely we'll get as far as the railroad."

To the others I said, "Let's not show any lights. Longer it takes them to discover we're up here the more chance we'll have of saying alive."

"We can't stumble about this damn place in the dark!" Harry snarled.

"We're going down to the next level—the one with the window holes—and that's where we'll stay. Careful now on that ladder. If you've got a pistol, Jones, I wish you'd stay up here for a bit till we're sure those Indians haven't found out we've come up here—but don't shoot anybody without you have to."

"Okay," Jones said, and edged past me. "It's blacker in here than the gut of a camel; can't see a hand in front of your face!"

"What good would it do you if you could?" Clampas asked from below.

"Can you catch hold of that dog, Jeff?" I called when he'd joined Clampas. "All right, Harry, you're next on the ladder. Now you, Fern," I said when Harry got off.

I left the ladder where it was after climbing down myself. "Have you got hold of Flossie, Jeff?"

"I've got her," Fern said.

"We don't want her running loose down below. Everything we want is on this level so keep a good hold on her till I scout up something to put over that hole."

Trouble was I could not recall seeing anything that would cover a hole three feet wide; the tent I reckoned would do very nicely but we hadn't fetched the tent. "Be better," Clampas said, "if we spread out, don't you think? Each of us pick out one of them window holes so we'll know where we're at. I'll take the one beyond the room with the chindis' hoard."

We could hear him moving off. Harry

said, cutting through the boot and spur sound, "I'll take the room this side of him," and went tramping off through the dark in the wake of his gunfighter. And this was when the dog slipped her collar and went scampering off in the same direction. "Flossie!" Fern called. "Come back here, Flossie!"

"I'll get her," Jeff growled and, when she refused to heed his whistle, went irascibly after her, muttering under his breath.

"Oh dear," Fern sighed. "She can be an awful nuisance . . ."

"Stay here," I said in the sudden grip of an unwanted thought. "Let me have that torch. Where are you?"

"Here—" she said, and put it into my hand, but before I could move we heard a yell and a thump and pitiful whimpering sounds out of Flossie.

CHAPTER TWENTY

Fern started off but I grabbed her. "Wait!"

"No!" She jerked loose of me. "Flossie's hurt—she needs me!"

I was too impatient, too crammed with the bitter black thoughts whirling through me,

207

to waste time arguing. I switched on the torch, went dashing through rooms, and to hell with the noise, caring only for getting there in the shortest time possible. Through the clattering beads, through the dark doorway, past the chindis' hoard and up to the floor hole where Harry and Clampas crouched peering into the black pit below.

I played the light down there, my worst fears realized, staring aghast at Jeff's crumpled shape and the dog whining beside him. "Looks," Clampas said, "like he's broken his neck."

I grabbed hold of Harry. "How'd it happen? Quick—tell me!"

But the man was too hysterical to get any sense out of him. I put the light onto Clampas. "It was the dog," Clampas said. "He was trying to catch hold of her and missed his footing . . ."

I looked a long while at him, hearing Fern come up and her gasped "Oh, God!"

Clampas said, quietly grim: "He *fell*, I tell you—I didn't push him. I was at the window when Flossie dashed past with Jeff racing after her and me diving after them, too late by ten strides. He was already down there when I got to the hole."

I blew out my breath, put an arm around

Fern. She was trembling all over, trying to stifle her sobs against my shoulder. I said, hating the necessity, "We'll have to leave him down there—for right now anyway. I'll bring up the dog." I slid my legs through the hole and let myself drop.

After making certain that Jeff was dead, and not just badly injured, I turned to the dog.

Flossie, still whimpering, must have understood more than you'd normally allow for, making no fuss when I hoisted her into Clampas's reaching hands. Clampas passed her to Fern and reached down for me. I got a knee over the hole and heaved myself up.

I thought later I should have shown Fern more sympathy in the shock of her loss, but at the time, right then, my head was too filled with the consequences and the needs they forced on me. At any moment now, with dawn scarce an hour from bursting over the horizon, that old man would be coming to demand a victim. I had to find some way to get us out of this trap; and I could see no way without a distraction.

I finally came up with a harebrained expedient, a notion so wild I damn near threw it away till I recalled Two-Feathers's words about the Navajos' sojourn at Bosque Redondo. Latching on to no alternative I reckoned it was better than nothing; not much but worth a try.

To Clampas I said, "Somewhere in one of the rooms on this level you'll find the barrel of my rifle and a coil of rope. Get them. There's an Anasazi flute, too; fetch me all three of them and don't waste no time."

I saw the speculative look that slid through his stare. He wasted no words but went off at once. Harry, I could see, would be of no use whatever. Fern was still holding Flossie when Clampas came back with the things I had asked for.

"Take a look out that window hole," I told him and, while he was doing it, I knotted one end of the rope round the rifle barrel, the way it had been when I found it. "How does it look?"

"Can't see anyone. You goin' down that rope?"

"If we're to get loose of this we've got to have some kind of distraction. Don't any of you try to leave till I come back. If I don't show inside of an hour you'll be on your own."

With the rifle barrel wedged the way I had found it I tossed the rope out the window. "Don't do it, Brice," Fern cried, her voice filled with alarm and her eyes big as saucers. "If you're seen they'll shoot you!"

"They're like to shoot all of us unless I'm able to come up with a diversion."

I thrust the flute in the grip of my waistband and catching hold of the rope thrust my feet through the window. Swinging around with feet keeping me clear of the wall I started down, hand under hand. Forty feet on that rope seemed more like forty miles with the expectation of being shot any moment. The horses in their pens were on my mind likewise but they were two miles away and almost certainly were watched.

Ten feet from the ground I let go of the rope and took off in great strides in the direction of the pool, flute in one hand and my shooting iron in the other. I was anxiously conscious of passing time but didn't dare run until I'd gained more distance. Fern was too right. If I was seen I'd be shot. When I figured I'd covered enough ground for safety I broke into a run.

I went through the trees around the pool without stopping, but slowed to a walk trying to catch me some breath and ease the cramp in my side. Five minutes later I stepped up my pace and, pretty quick then, I started running again. It seemed like when

I quit I must have covered about five miles. I stretched out on the ground till I caught up with myself, rummaging my memories, recalling my youthful admiration of the boys in blue.

When I got my wind back I scrambled erect and, grabbing up the flute, blew the cavalry charge. Loud and clear it sailed through the dawn, not quite like a bugle, but near enough for a Navajo. Then at a limping run I started back and ten minutes later with the sun throwing my shadow long ahead of me I sounded the cavalry's get-up call.

At last, within two miles of the cliff house I put the Anasazi flute to my lips and blared out the cavalry charge again.

I moved with a deal more caution now, eyes skinned sharp for the first hint of trouble. I had done what I could but was afraid deep inside it would not fool an old man sharp as Johnny Two-Feathers. I watched every rock, every bush and shadow, eyes strained to catch the least blur of movement. I still had the flute and the sweat creeping cold down the length of my spine when I rounded the last bend and saw the cliff house before me.

Clampas spotted me at once and came sliding down the rope. "Corrigan, you're a wonder—you really are! That flute cleared them out of here, lock, stock an' barrel!"

"How about our horses?"

"They didn't stop to grab'em. I sent Jones out to look."

"We've got a chance then," I said, "and that's all we've got. No time to fool around. They'll be back just as soon as they discover they've been tricked, and they'll be looking for blood."

He considered me brightly. "What about that turquoise?"

"If it was up to me I'd leave it. After losing her brother I guess Fern will not be wanting to leave any of the stuff that cost him his life. They brought a bunch of sacks, I remember. We'll take whatever they'll hold and no more. When they're packed we'll let them down on that rope, pick'em up here after we get the horses."

I was right about Fern. She wanted the pots they'd set aside, all the turquoise and several bones. I said, "Be reasonable, Fern. We can't take all that stuff. We oughtn't take any of it. Those Indians will be back, and damn soon probably."

Ignoring this she said, "And I want that

stone lamp Jeff's been carrying in his pocket—we'll have to take him, too."

I shook my head, seeing the futility of argument. "We'll put the stuff in those burlap sacks—"

"You can't put Jeff in a sack!" she flared. "Anyway there are no sacks up here."

I reminded myself of her loss and the shock and kept my temper where it belonged. Just the same, with my experience of Indians and time running out, I was just about ready to jump out of my skin.

Jones came down from his lookout. "You want I should fix us some grub?"

"We got no time to be lallygaggin' around. Go fetch me those sacks from the stores we carried up—and I mean right now. Stir your stumps!"

"Where's Flossie?" I said to Fern.

"She's around here somewhere—"

"Damnation!" I swore as my glance lit on Harry. "What the hell have you got in your pockets?"

He backed away from me shaking. His left eye twitched. "I only done what Clampas told me—"

"You turd!" Clampas snarled. "Anything I want I'm big enough to carry!"

Fern, paying no attention to this, was

moving jugged turquoise from one place to another. Exasperated I said, "Never noticed before that you were into Jeff's line—"

"Enough of it's rubbed off for me to know what's worth saving . . . I want that flute, too! If we could I'd take back one of those skeletons; never mind how I feel about them. Bound to be a demand for anything that old."

"Most of the horses we're going to have to use aren't pack animals. They'll be the devil to load and there's a limit to how much they'll carry. We'd do a damn sight better to be riding them."

Clampas, I noticed, was eyeing Fern distastefully. I said, "Get over to that aperture and keep your eyes on the prowl for them Indians. You better pull up that rope. . . ."

Jones came in with an armload of sacks. "Fine," I told him. "You can help Fern fill them," and catching up one of those burlaps myself I began dumping jugs of turquoise into it. "You'll have that all mixed up!" Fern cried censoriously.

"We haven't the time to pick and choose—you should have done all that yesterday! Can't you get it through your female head a Navajo's just as human as you are?

They'll be back here full of sound an' fury—"

"Company comin'," Clampas called from his aperture. "Good God A'mighty! Come look what's down there!"

I flung over there. Some jasper was sitting down there in a buggy like a syndicate ranch boss, all togged out in his big-city duds. "Who the hell's that?" I snarled at Clampas.

"Hello up there!" this dude chucked at us. "What do you people think you're doing?"

"Fishin'," Clampas told him. "What's it to you?"

"D'you know who I am?" He sounded plumb riled. "Happens I'm the Inspector of Antiquities for the sovereign people of New Mexico. How'd you get into that place? It was sealed up tighter than a boar's ass! Don't you know you're violating the law?"

"Do tell," Clampas said.

"I'm gettin' out of here!" Harry declared through chattering teeth.

"Get down on your hunkers and help fill these sacks!" I gave him a shove. "And you can empty those pockets into one of them too."

"That joker still down there?" I snarled at Clampas.

"Sure is—can't you hear him?"

"Them horses," I told Jones, "must be bustin' for water. Get down there and see to it."

I had so much on my mind I couldn't think straight. That jasper in the buggy called up to say, "All the old ruins in and around Chaco Canyon have been declared off-limits to vandals and all you pot-hunting buggers. By rights I ought to take you people—"

"By rights," I yelled, sticking my head out the aperture, "if you don't get out of there in one tearin' big rush you're like to find your hair on a Navajo lance!"

"New Mexico's at peace with the Navajo Nation. Those redskins have been pacified—"

"Stick around awhile and you'll learn how peaceful and pacified they are." I told Clampas to get that rope tied around a couple sacks and start them on down. "We've got to hustle this up and get out of here"

That old fool in the buggy was still shooting his jaw off. "Breaking into this property will probably get you three to ten with— Here, you! What's on that rope? You can get ten years if you're caught looting a ruin—Haul that back up!"

"Get it down there," I told Clampas, and

stuck my head out the aperture. "Be a gent for a change," I told the goggling bureaucrat, "and unloose that rope so we can pull it back up. We got a lot more to go and time's gettin' short."

He peered as if he was staring at a two-headed calf. "Get at it," I said, "before you catch a blue whistler," and thrust the front end of Clampas's Sharps out where he could see it.

He couldn't believe it. I shifted the muzzle till it was looking right at him. Red-faced and spluttering, he got out of his buggy, and bent over the sacks.

I hauled up the rope and lashed a couple more onto it.

It was while this second batch were on their way down that Fern clamped a hand on me. "Listen!" she cried, the freckles showing up like splatters of paint. "Don't you *hear* it?"

"I hear it."

In the blazing wrath of that midday sun there was a quality that made the blood run cold in the sound of those throbbing drums.

CHAPTER TWENTY-ONE

"Navajos?"

"You bet." I yelled at the dude, "Catch hold of that rope and we'll haul you up."

He stood there like something built out of matchsticks. Fern shook my arm. "What are we going to *do?*"

"They're comin' back!" Harry gasped. Way he was shaking it was a wonder he was able to stay in his clothes.

I called down to the dude, "Tie the rope around you under your arms and grab on to it." He was about as stupid as a newborn sheep. "Hurry it up!" I yelled; when he finally got fixed we started reeling him in. He was no featherweight with all that soft living but we got him up with a face like spoiled putty, and Clampas hauled him in through the aperture.

Fern shook my arm again. "If we left right now couldn't we still get away?"

I said with some hope, "We'd have a chance anyway. Grab your hat and—"

"But I've still got some of those things to be packed and somebody will have to fetch that stone lamp and—"

"You can't leave right now and do forty-'leven other things! Make up your mind. It's either one or the other. Forget the rest of it. You'll have enough turquoise—"

"Oh, I couldn't—How could I abandon the result of all Jeff's work! How can you ask me to?" She looked around distractedly. "And I *did* want to take poor Jeff with us. If I can't he'll have to be buried . . . I hate to leave him in this horrible place. . . ."

"All right. Now we know where we're at, I hope. Best chance left is for the jasper who croaked that smartass Indian to own up to it and take his medicine." I looked at them, disgusted when no one rushed forward to take the blame. "Then all that's left if you want to keep breathin'—"

The dude, looking horrified, broke in to say, "Did I hear correctly someone needs to be buried?"

"My brother," Fern said.

"What did he die of?—By the way, my name's Witherspoon."

"I understand he fell through a hole in one of the floors," I told him, impatient.

"Broke his neck," Clampas said.

Jones came through the doorhole this side of the beads. I said, astonished, "Thought you'd gone to the pool with the horses?"

"Well . . ." Jones fetched up a sick-looking grin. "When them drums got to poundin' it didn't seem advisable to get that far from shelter. I used up what we had left in the water bags, lettin' them guzzle it outa my hat."

"You see any Navajos?"

"Didn't see any, no; but I bet they seen me."

"See Flossie anyplace?"

"Came past her in that room with the sandpile; didn't see no cat but she was diggin' like she figured one was in it."

"Come on, Fern." I gave her a nudge. "We'd better get hold of her."

"I'll go with you," said Witherspoon promptly, and ran a jaundiced look over me. "I gather you're the head of this 'scientific' expedition?"

"Just a hired hand."

"My brother, Professor Larrimore, was head of it," Fern told him. "This dig was—"

"Just where is this dig? You been digging in here?"

"Jeff never got around to—"

"We've had a heap of hard luck," I butted in to say. "One damn thing after another. Now, with you jumping in—"

"Great Scott!" Witherspoon gasped, staring in astonished dismay at what our Flossie had uncovered in that sandpile. I wouldn't be surprised to learn my own jaw dropped. For there in the midst of that pile of loose sand stood three medium-sized jars of perhaps the finest cut stones of spiderweb turquoise I had ever laid eyes on.

"Get a sack, Brice," Fern said crisply. "The regents will be delighted with the display they can make of this. And these Anasazi jars—"

"I forbid you, madam, to remove one piece of that off these premises!"

That hoity-toity dude was all swelled up like a carbuncle, crammed with the righteous wrath of his office. "I will remind you of the law. The law unequivocally states that any person digging or carrying off relics and/or artifacts of any nature whatsoever from terrain protected by the State of New Mexico—"

I caught his eye, jerked my head toward the door, beckoning him after me into the next room. He came reluctantly and even more reluctantly listened eventually to what I decided to tell him. It was plain he didn't like it and stood there spluttering like a batch of damp firecrackers. "I don't care at all for your attitude, young man, and if that's a threat . . ."

"Just a promise," I said, and went to fetch Fern a sack.

It was astonishing the way that girl had recovered from the loss of "poor" Jeff. She appeared to have taken on a whole new character, I thought with just a shade of resentment. Doubtless this was just her real self emerging after years of standing in the shadow of an ambitious brother. Looked like she had made up her mind to step into his shoes and reap any credit she could from this trip.

This didn't come over me all at once, you understand. The notion just sort of grew on me. Right then I wasn't doing much thinking with the sound of those drums steadily banging through my head. I reckoned to have Witherspoon stymied for a spell, but getting around old Johnny and his braves was a horse of a different color.

On the way back to Fern with the sack Jones caught hold of me. "You set that gasbag down in a hurry." Still eyeing me curious, he asked, "Are we goin' for the broncs? I'd like to get the hell out of here."

I sighed. "So would I."

"That girl got the bit in her teeth?"

"Looks that way. She wants to take all the pots and at least a few bones. Fact is she's honin' to pack one of those dead Basketmakers Clampas dug up down in that cliff shelter—"

"We can't take the time to pack—"

"What I told her. Be lucky to get away with that turquoise, but she's some set on it."

"Why don't you put your foot down?"

It didn't come easy but I managed a grin. "Want to try your luck?"

"I'm just the cook. She wouldn't pay me no mind."

"Me neither," I said. "Grab up a couple more of them sacks."

When we got back to Fern she said, "I'm glad you fetched those extra sacks. We'll wrap them around these jars and leave the stones inside them."

We did just that. I gave the sack to Jones and told him to send it down on the rope. "Then you and Clampas head for the horses—"

Fern said, "Don't forget that stone lamp Jeff's got in his pocket."

"Yes, ma'am. I'm going down right now to pick it up." Giving her a servant's look, I inquired, "Will there be anything else? How about one of those skeletons?"

She gave me a rueful smile. "I'm reasonably sure those skeletons are the most important finds we've made. I hate not being able to take at least one."

Clampas, at that moment joining us, said, "Them Injuns might be downright uncivil if they caught us luggin' off one of their ancestors."

She appeared a bit startled. "I hadn't thought of that. Anyway it doesn't seem practical . . . unless Mr. Witherspoon would take it in his buggy."

"Better ask him." Clampas smiled. "Seems to be a real obligin' sort."

I limped over to the floor hole and down the ladder, dug through Jeff's pockets and, lifting his wallet in addition to the lamp, fetched them back to Fern with another of the bones Flossie had been playing with. "Let's go."

Out on the clifftop with the sun bearing down and that goddam drumming still banging up a storm, the only movement I could see came from Jones, Clampas and that fatass Witherspoon picking their way down through the rockfall. No sign of a redskin, I was relieved to note. I couldn't set much hope on that since you seldom ever spot one till they're about to lift your hair.

Ten minutes later Fern and I reached the rockfall and, at that precise moment, the drums went silent. A whole flock of wild thoughts fluttered through my head and the sweat turned cold underneath my hat.

"Look!" Fern cried.

I didn't need any coaching. I'd already seen them. Half the Navajo Nation, it looked like, spread out across the opposite bluff.

CHAPTER TWENTY-TWO

"Never mind," I said. "I'll get you out of this."

She twisted her head about, looking appalled. "Brice—I can't let you *do* this!"

"We'll see. Just remember one thing: when you're free to go, by God you *go*. Understand? No lallygaggin' round. You make one stop. At the tamarisks, and don't let those caballos drink too much. Fill the water bags and get the hell out of there."

She looked rebellious with her chin up that way. But I nudged her along. "Worst thing you can do is let those Navajos think you're afraid. Remember how upset you were to think that old man had to sleep on the ground?" I managed a laugh, and nudged her on ahead of me, wishing I felt as confident as she thought me.

Old Johnny was waiting for me there by the pens.

Before we could speak the fat Inspector of Antiquities came bustling up to him, puffed up with importance and the authority of his office. "My name's Witherspoon. I guess you know I speak for the Government? Yes—yes indeed! Our Great White Father up in Washington has much admiration for our Navajo friends and has appointed me to look after their best interests . . ."

"Lucky Navajos!" Clampas muttered in back of me someplace. Myself, I was trying to think how best I could put what I had to say to this red brother who was a heap less simple than Witherspoon thought him. One thing was sure: this old rascal hadn't forgotten what he had come for or how he'd been balked of his prey once already.

With an expressionless face old Johnny sliced through the rhetoric with a lifted hand. "My business here is with Man-on-a-Mule."

Fern and Flossie, I saw, were with Turtle

Jones some thirty or forty feet back of Clampas—far enough off, it was my devout hope, not to latch on to what I aimed to say. I didn't want it spoiled by any words out of her. Two-Feathers faced me with some asperity. "Speak, Man-on-a-Mule!"

"You're here," I said, "for the man responsible for the death of Hosteen Joe. We're prepared to give him up if I have your assurance the rest of our party will then be free to leave this place."

"Where this man?"

"Do I have your assurance?"

I watched his glance passing over our company and settle on me with a long, searching look. And at last, reluctantly, he nodded. "Where this man?"

"He is in the old cliff dwelling."

"Why you not bring?"

I could read the suspicion abruptly staring from his glance.

"Well . . ." I dredged up a sigh with a rueful look. "I couldn't get him out of there."

"We get. You show."

He looked again at Clampas, at Jones and the girl with her hold on Flossie's collar. Once more he nodded, and to them said,

"You go." And then, as an afterthought: "One horse each."

"Two ponies," I said, shaking my head.

Despite what I'd told her, Fern of course had to put in her oar, stubbornly declaring, "I'm not about to go unless you're going too!"

"Be quiet," I growled, scared the whole thing would start to unravel. "I'll catch up with you later." To the old man I said, "Two ponies. They're going home—have to catch iron horse."

Those Navajo eyes never left my face but thin of lip he nodded. "Agreed."

Clampas, Jones, Witherspoon and a whey-faced Hatcher went into the pens and fetched out ten horses, on one of which, under Johnny's watchful eye, they packed a sack of tinned food, our eating tools, and the washtub. Then they all mounted up and with Flossie in the lead started off down the gulch on the trail to Chaco Canyon.

Beckoning several of his warriors down from the bluff, Johnny eyeing me reflectively commanded, "You show. Now."

So I limped off on foot up the climb through the rockfall nervously wondering if this would be the last time. I couldn't hear those redskins but knew they wouldn't be far behind. "Who this man?" grunted Johnny, directly back of me.

I told him it was Larrimore, boss and organizer of this field trip.

"The great scientist friend of the Navajo?"

"Yeah."

"Why he shoot Hosteen Joe?"

"Joe had a rifle one of the others had given him. Larrimore didn't like it."

"For one rifle he kill Joe?"

Pretty weak, I thought, but said, "Looks that way. He's no great hand for explanations."

When we got to the entrance we had made getting in there the old man motioned me into the lead, alertly following my snug passage through the hole. "Bad. Bad," he grumbled. "Chindis not like."

When I mentioned we had no torch he gobbled out something unintelligible to me and one of his clan disappeared to return with an armful of creosote brush from which several torches were speedily fashioned. Each of these men he'd picked to accompany him had a rifle and three of them wore bandoliers of cartridges. I reckoned he was determined to exact his due, and again the cold chill of this place crept over me, not lessened in the least by the thought of his outrage when he finally confronted the man I had promised him.

I took as long as I could guiding him to this denouement. When we got to the hole through which Jeff had plunged he ordered a torch lit and in its flare stared, it seemed like forever, at the crumpled shape below.

CHAPTER TWENTY-THREE

At last he looked at me. "White man cheat."

I'd had plenty of time to think about this and, for what it was worth, had my answer ready. "Not at all," I said. "You demanded Joe's killer but nothing was mentioned about him having to be alive."

"Why you kill?"

"I wasn't there when he died. I was told he'd been chasing the dog, lost his footing in the dark and plunged through the hole."

"This is true?"

"I can only say they didn't want the dog in the lower levels. It seems logical to believe it might have happened that way."

He looked at me hard. "What you do with these people? Why you not with Ranger?"

"Ain't Ranger now—leg caught a bullet.

Was on my way home when I ran into the Larrimores. They were afraid of the crew hired for them by Hatcher." A little edge of bitterness got into my voice when I said, "They thought I could protect them."

He told the rest of them what I had said and it was plain by the angry sound of their gobbling they were determined I should pay for my duplicity. Strange as it may seem the old man stood out against them. When they finally buttoned their lips he said to me with an unshakable dignity, "The Navajo is an honorable man. I not like what you do, Man-on-a-Mule, but my word is good. This time you go. I have spoken."

The sun was low down above the western rim when I got back to the camp and limped over to the pen and dropped my hull on her, kneed the air from her belly, yanked the girth tight and climbed wearily aboard. There was a saying among Mossman's men that a Ranger was a man who never looked back. I set my jaw and put Gretchen down the trail.

Pausing briefly at the pool by the tamarisks I let her have a short drink and then sent her along at her rough-gaited trot with little expectation of overtaking Fern's party this side of night.

There had been no sacks below the cliff house when I'd passed, with them so burdened it seemed fairly obvious I'd come up with them at my faster pace before they reached the Chaco.

About an hour after dark I heard the rattle and skreak of Witherspoon's buggy not a great ways ahead of me. When we drew alongside I motioned for him to pull up and, when he had done so, asked if he'd any oats under the seat.

"Well, yes," he admitted, "but not any more than I'll be needing myself."

"Pass them over. My need," I said, "is greater than yours and Mossman will reimburse you on my note of hand."

"You're way out of your jurisdiction, Corrigan."

I scribbled him a note and tossed it into his lap. "Reckon that's so." I gave him a look at my pistol. "Let's not waste any time over this."

Grumbling and spluttering dire threats he surrendered the sack. Settling it in front of me I told him I was obliged and left him still fuming.

Fern and company had made better time

than I'd ever expected, packing all the weight of that turquoise. Flossie let out a wild series of barks before I caught sight of them in the moon-dappled shadows perhaps two miles short of the canyon. The others pulled up in a bunch when the dog ran to meet us with Fern right behind. And the first thing Fern said was, "Brice! How'd you ever get away from them? Of course! You must have given them Jeff . . ."

"Yes. He was the only one they couldn't reach."

"But wasn't Johnny furious?"

"I expect he was; but with Navajos, Fern, a deal is a deal and the old man was stuck with it. Where's Clampas?"

"Gone," she said. There was a world of bitterness in that bleak voice. "Gone with every last ounce of our turquoise!"

Well, I thought, I should have expected this. "How long?"

"Pretty close to an hour . . ."

"Never mind. I'll catch him. He'll be heading for the railroad at Farmington." And without further words I set out after him.

With any kind of luck I reckoned to overtake him before he was able to get out of Chaco

Canyon. That was the first thing that crossed my mind. But before I had gone more than a whoop and a holler other thoughts latched on to me. Like he might, at this point, have no intention of busting out of the canyon. He was sure to figure I'd be right on his tail.

Given this situation what, I wondered, would I do in his place? He had all the advantage, knowing me as he did. Always big Clampas was a man for the edge. Brave as a lion, audacious but never reckless. Slicker than slobbers. I could see, thinking that way, he was going to hole up. Hole up someplace with that goddam Sharps and let me come to him.

Without hideous risk I'd no way to get near him. Long as he could keep me out of pistol range he could tease me the way a cat does a mouse, and enjoy every minute of it. Even if I waited for the others to come up it wouldn't change the odds enough to matter. Harry, back when he was riding high, had taken the rifles away from us peons; and then, after Fletch had been killed, Clampas had become the he-catawampus and leached all the courage Hatcher'd ever had out of him.

I had known all along Clampas was the deadly one. Even though, for my money, he'd eliminated Alfredo, Fletcher, Hosteen Joe and then Jeff, I'd nothing but my own belief—not so much as a scrap of proof. Which was why he'd been getting so much pleasure out of me. He'd known I was on to him, known I couldn't touch him. And he hadn't made the least effort to conceal from me that no matter the odds, he meant to have every bit of that turquoise. And now he had it!

I found it a mighty humiliating fact.

Nor was I able to work up any great enthusiasm for playing six-shooter tag through some ruin's empty rooms, for there again all the edge lay with Clampas. Ambush was his stock in trade.

As was happening all too frequent of late a picture of Fern with her roan hair and freckles came into my mind with a poignant clarity I could not deny. I thought if things had been different . . . and dismissed such empty dreams with an oath.

I kicked my thoughts back where they belonged, centered squarely on Clampas. A glib, wryly humorous, slippery villain to whom fair play was nothing but a laugh.

Already Gretchen had carried me past several ruins and a glance at the heavens assured me it would not be long before daylight would give him, with that Sharps, an additional edge. I began watching for tracks that turned away from the trail, went the best part of another mile before locating any that seemed sufficiently fresh. When I did come on to some they went angling away toward another ruined pueblo. He'd be holed up inside, squatting like some obscene spider, waiting for me to come into his sights.

I thought there had to be some other way to get at him, some way to cut down the advantage of that Sharps. If I could find his horses . . .

I cut away from his tracks, aiming to circle this ruin—it was one of the larger ones—at a distance hopefully sufficient to ensure my safety. I was thinking also of Gretchen; I couldn't afford to lose her in so desolate a place.

We got about halfway around those crumbling walls, towering in some spots almost fifty feet high, before in a patch of still, deep shadow I made out what I took to be the horses I was hunting. Those were horses all right; a questioning whinny confirmed this. Before she could answer I clamped a hand on Gretchen's nostrils.

Now what to do?

It was entirely probable Clampas was as

aware of that whinny as I was. He might not be able to see me yet. Should I make an attempt—with the attendant risks—of trying to drive those horses away? Leave him afoot and force him to move? But with the size of this place I could see right away such a notion was foolish. Then another occurred to me that seemed a heap better. Grab the horses if I could and light out for the railroad, reverse our positions and force Clampas to be the hunter.

There was, I figured, considerable merit in this notion. For unless he could get himself mounted again I could be at the railroad a good piece ahead of him.

But the thought of that Sharps in this growing light put a cold chill through this jubilant thinking. That sonofabitch would knock Gretchen from under me sure as God made little green apples! Fond as I was of her, it wasn't this that deterred me but the knowledge he could then pick me off at his leisure.

Any jasper who could shoot a flipped penny into oblivion was not to be taken lightly.

Turning Gretchen ever more away from where those whinnying horses stood I went on with the circling inspection I had started.

In about ten minutes the sun would be up. Whatever I decided was going to have to be done quickly. I could picture Clampas crouched in there someplace grinning over the sights of that Sharps, chuckling while he waited with Indian patience for me to move into range.

Some forty yards farther along I saw a whaleback rock with a fringe of greasewood some thirty feet closer to the battered walls than where I sat Gretchen, and the sight of this put a new aspect before me. The rock rose perhaps two feet above the shale-strewn surface of the ground all about it.

The possibilities this opened up were simply too tempting for me to resist. I got off the mule and considered it some more while I ran a hand across the loops of my belt, finding plenty of cartridges for what I had in mind.

The next step, of course, was how to reach it alive and in reasonable working order.

I didn't want to sacrifice Gretchen. Nor did I want to catch one of that Sharps's blue whistlers. I thought about it some more and moved Gretchen back a bit and sat down cross-legged to study it in depth, hoping these tactics might prod Clampas's temper or maybe stretch his nerves a little.

I gave it another five minutes and without more ado, with the rock between me and where I hoped he might be, I got over on my belly and began to wriggle toward its shelter.

Wham! went the Sharps and a lead plum went skittering off the rock's rounded top. He tried a couple more with no better result and by that time I was snuggled up against it. I blew out a held breath and sleeved the sweat off my forehead.

I had him placed now, but no guarantee he would stay there. Near as I could tell, without seeking a new and even more distant position, there seemed no way he'd be able to flank me. Breaking off four or five of the greasewood shoots, in time-honored fashion I edged the crown of my hat a very tiny way above the rock and Clampas promptly drilled it. He must have guessed the hat was empty; just wanted to show me what he could do. Or perhaps he was getting a little mite edgy. After all, he had to know the others would soon be along and he couldn't watch more than one place at a time. While Clampas was dealing with me, Jones and possibly Harry could slip into that ruin and make his position untenable.

While these thoughts were scampering around I had worked off my shirt and stuffed the top part of it with greasewood branches. Shoving another down through these I set my hat on it and poked this scarecrow enough above my shelter to entice two rapid reports. Both shots scored and as the dummy collapsed I let out a scream that should have sounded pretty desperate.

With much care I got back into my shirt and composed myself to wait for his foot-steps.

But Clampas, too wily to let go of his advantage, put in no appearance.

The sun climbed higher. It began to get hot. My ears ached from listening for sounds that never came. An almost irresistible impulse urged me to move and only the knowledge of what it might cost kept me motionless. Certainly I could show as much patience as Clampas so long as those horses stayed where I could see them.

I could, I supposed, afford a bit more. Bothered by flies those horses were beginning to get restive and Clampas must know this; he must know too that the companions he'd robbed at gunpoint were bound pretty soon to be coming along.

I wasn't surprised when those fretting horses began to drift off. Now, I thought, he's going to have to make a move. With extreme caution I took a quick look around the end of my rock. Nothing happened, nor did I see him. My exploring hand found a piece of flat shale—the kind we used to skip across ponds—and scaled it, cursing, at the ruin's nearest wall.

CHAPTER TWENTY-FOUR

Everything seemed to happen at once.

A rumble of hoofs came up from the trail. Clampas crashed another shot whining off my rock. The confiscated horses he had lifted from our outfit, filled now with a whinnying excitement, went tearing off to rejoin their companions, turquoise and all. Clampas came over the broken wall of his refuge as though flung from a catapult, making straight for me, triggering that Sharps at every jump. How he missed hitting me I've never been able to understand. Only Burt Mossman's drilled-in discipline kept me rock-steady in the face of that charge. When he got near enough I fanned off one shot which must have caught him head-on. Arms flung out, he spun half around and collapsed in his tracks.

I saw Fern's mop of roan hair driving

through milling horses, Jones's rigid face and Harry's frightened one, and then they were around me, all talking at once, and creating such bedlam it made my head swim, and I thought this must be what hell was like.

When finally I began to function once more I began looking for Gretchen and found her trying to lift her head off the ground. As through a fog I stumbled over to where she lay with those great loyal eyes staring up at me. I fumbled a sugar lump out of my pocket and patted her shoulder. "You were a real lady, Gretchen," I told her, and put my pistol against her head.

When my surroundings came into true focus again Jones was putting my saddle on one of the horses. "Guess we're about ready," he said handing me the reins. "I've put the sacks on three of our spares. You want to lead off?"

"I suppose so. Keep your eye on Harry —he doesn't have a gun, does he? Good. You and him better ride drag; we don't want to lose any of those loose mounts between here and Farmington. We've got thirty-odd miles still ahead of us."

I rode more or less like I wasn't all there till Fern came up with some more conversation, none of which registered till she said, looking around at me, "I guess you couldn't have saved her?"

I didn't want to gab about it. "She got one of those slugs in the neck. Another broke a leg."

We rode for a while without further talk, which was one blessing anyway. But she was too full of plans and excitement to have kept her notions to herself for long. She kept twisting her head with her blue-green eyes slanching probing glances in my direction and then, unable longer to remain bottled up, declared, "I haven't yet thanked you for saving that stuff—"

"No thanks necessary," I cut into it brusquely.

"Well, you needn't bite my head off! How long will it take us to get to the railroad?"

"It's around thirty miles from where we are now. We'll have to camp out tonight. With a good deal of luck we might reach Farmington tomorrow—late."

"Couldn't we just push right on?"

"These horses," I said, "ain't made of iron, Fern. They've got to have rest."

"But with these spares to switch off on—"

"Unless you're prepared to hoof it and leave all your booty."

"Oh, I couldn't do that—I mean give up that turquoise, those bones and the lamp."

"Then we camp out tonight," I said with finality.

And that's what we did.

Seemed like we were all more worn out than we'd been ready to admit. The sun was just creeping over those distant hills with Shiprock looming blue-gray against the brightening sky when Jones roused us out to eat our refried beans, sloshed down with java.

We were loading the horses when Jones grabbed my arm, swinging me around to follow the lift of his hand toward where a column of smoke pale gray in the sunlight was rising above a distant mesa. Even as we watched we saw the smoke cut off. Then three quick puffs shot skyward after it. Flossie was looking up at us nervously.

"Signals?" He looked to be in a state of shock. I met his rounded stare and nodded, telling myself I wasn't filled with the jumps but knowing damn well I was and couldn't help it. I was about to tell him to keep his mouth shut, but Harry's alarmed cry caught Fern's attention and I saw her cheeks turn gray as she took in the last of that disappearing haze.

"You don't suppose that's Navajos, do you?"

"Could be Pueblos," I said with professed indifference.

But she'd spotted another smoke off to the west and conviction showed in the shape of her stare.

I said to Jones, "Let's get this outfit on the road," and we hustled things up and presently were riding into the morning's strengthening heat. No one but Harry felt inclined for gab. With a twitch in his cheek and his eyes looking wild, he yelled at me, "I thought you'd fixed things up with that sonofabitch!"

"We don't know that it's them. Even if it is, those puffadillies may not concern us at all."

And Fern said, hopeful through stiffened lips, "If Johnny's bunch had changed their minds they'd have caught us up hours ago. Before we had even got out of the canyon."

"That's right," I put in, but couldn't help thinking Johnny's mind had been changed for him, remembering those furious faces at the cliff house.

The morning wore along with the sun glaring down with increasing malevolence and me holding the horses down to what they could handle in this increasing heat and given our shortage of water.

Now and again we saw additional smokes in the hazy distance and when Fern's look grew agitated I said, "They're just making sure we get out of the country." But I didn't believe it and she didn't either.

We stopped at noon to shift the loads and Jones broke open two tins of corned beef, the contents of which we choked down in silence while all of us covertly kept tabs on the skyline.

"You know what it is," Harry kept muttering, "they're after the chindis' horde, that's what!"

At last I said, fed up with his whining, "If you reckon you can do better, cut loose and take off."

I could see the hate shining bright in his stare. "I ain't leavin' without my pay."

"Your performance with this outfit doesn't merit any pay. You've been nothing but a drag ever since you signed, not to mention your sundry treacheries!"

Fern dug out Jeff's wallet. "I'll pay him—"

"Pay him nothing," I growled, and we rode on through the heat and the vast silence of this waste that grew nothing that lived but the gray wands of wolf's candle.

The hours dragged. The heat pulled sweat out of us that was dried by the ovenlike atmosphere before it could drip. By midafternoon with the sentinel peak of Shiprock much plainer, Harry, forever twisting for frightened looks behind, suddenly cried in a panic, "There's a dust back there!"

Without bothering to look I said disparagingly, "Nothing but a twister. What you dudes call a dust devil. In this kind of country you get'em all the time."

"I don't think so, Corrigan. I been keepin' my eye on it. Them's horses that's stirrin' it." He took another look. "Might be cavalry."

"Might be jumpin' beans," I said, disgusted.

Fern said, "Can't we go a little faster?"

I licked dry lips. "Whatever it is we're not going to lose it by killin' these horses. If it's Navajos they know this region a sight better than we do. They ride light. They don't pack forty-pound saddles or half a ton of turquoise—not to mention pots and bones!"

CHAPTER TWENTY-FIVE

Knowing it was useless but under pressure from those hairy looks I did step up the pace a bit and on we went, worried, brooding, our anxiety increasing with each passing mile.

The horses were beginning to show the strain, especially the ones burdened with packs, all of them seeming more gaunt than I liked. We weren't, I figured, above six miles from the rails but it might as well have been sixty when Harry cried out, "It's them Navajos—I *knew* it! I can see them plain!"

Stood to reason, of course. But, I thought, if we could manage to get within sight of the town there was still a thin chance they'd give it up and pull off. I was coddling this notion when Jones growled on an outblown breath, "There's dust up ahead—they've cut us off!"

"It doesn't have to be Indians," Fern said, voice reedy, and slung a look at me. "Couldn't it be cavalry?"

"Not again," I said; and Jones, in no mood for a laugh, told her, "Ain't no cavalry around these parts."

I said, "We've pretty near run that dog off

her legs. We might's well stop and get it over with."

Nobody liked it but only Jones spoke. "Might's well," he said grimly.

We pulled up. "No gunplay," I said.

"I guess," Fern admitted, "this dig of Jeff's was star-crossed from the start," and I nodded. "Sure does seem so, looking back. An exercise in futility, doomed from the time he signed Harry on."

"I wish," Fern said, "I'd thought to keep out that stone lamp, or one of the bones Flossie dug up to play with. If their dating coincided with Jeff's theories the regents might allow me to return next year, even if they put someone else in charge. Those seven skeletons—"

I said, "I guess we can give the poor dog a bone." Dismounting, I limped over to the horse that was carrying the lightest pack, the one she'd put those three jars into, fished out the leg bone and tossed it to Flossie. Though she made no move to catch it, and with her tongue lolling out a foot and forty inches, she did condescend to drop down beside it. Thoughtfully eyeing me, Fern said, "I wonder if I could someway manage to hang on to those jars . . ."

I shook my head, too used up even to grin.

It didn't take the Navajos long to surround us; I'd have been glad right then of a few covered wagons, considering the uproar. They closed in from all sides waving a miscellany of weapons, gobbling up a storm. Old Two-Feathers let them holler, then shut it off with a lifted hand.

Looking over our sorry company, looking especially and longest at the horse I was hunkered by, he said, "Man-Without-Mule, we meet again."

"Ain't that a fact? Thought you told me we were free to go?"

"To go, yes. But not with things that belong to the chindis. I personally, as our white brothers say, will care for these venerated relics," he smiled, "as though they were my own."

I smiled too. "I believe you will."

Johnny Two-Feathers nodded. "Make much jewelry." Then he waved a hand and the whole band headed back to the Chaco with our packhorses and packs.

"Well," Fern said, "we've still got each other," and Flossie, bright eyes peering up at us, wriggled and wagged in plainest approval.

ArB W.

5→